DRAGONSDALE

DRAGON

NSDALE

SALAMANDA DRAKE

Illustrations by
GILLY MARKLEW

Chicken House

SCHOLASTIC INC./NEW YORK

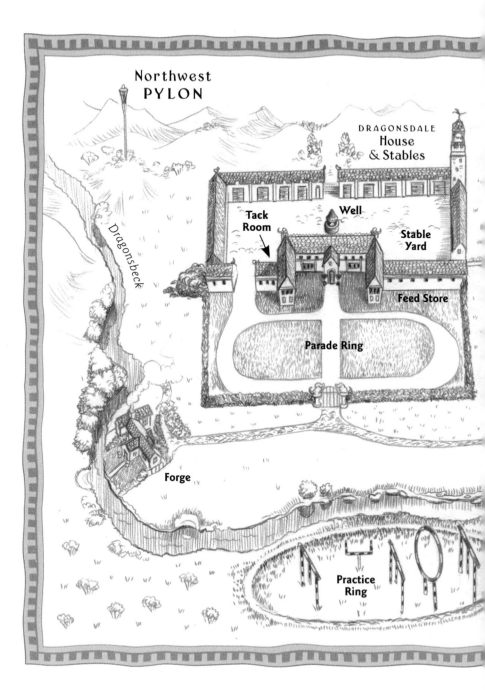

Northwest
PYLON

DRAGONSDALE
House
& Stables

Dragonsbeck

Tack
Room

Well

Stable
Yard

Feed Store

Parade Ring

Forge

Practice
Ring

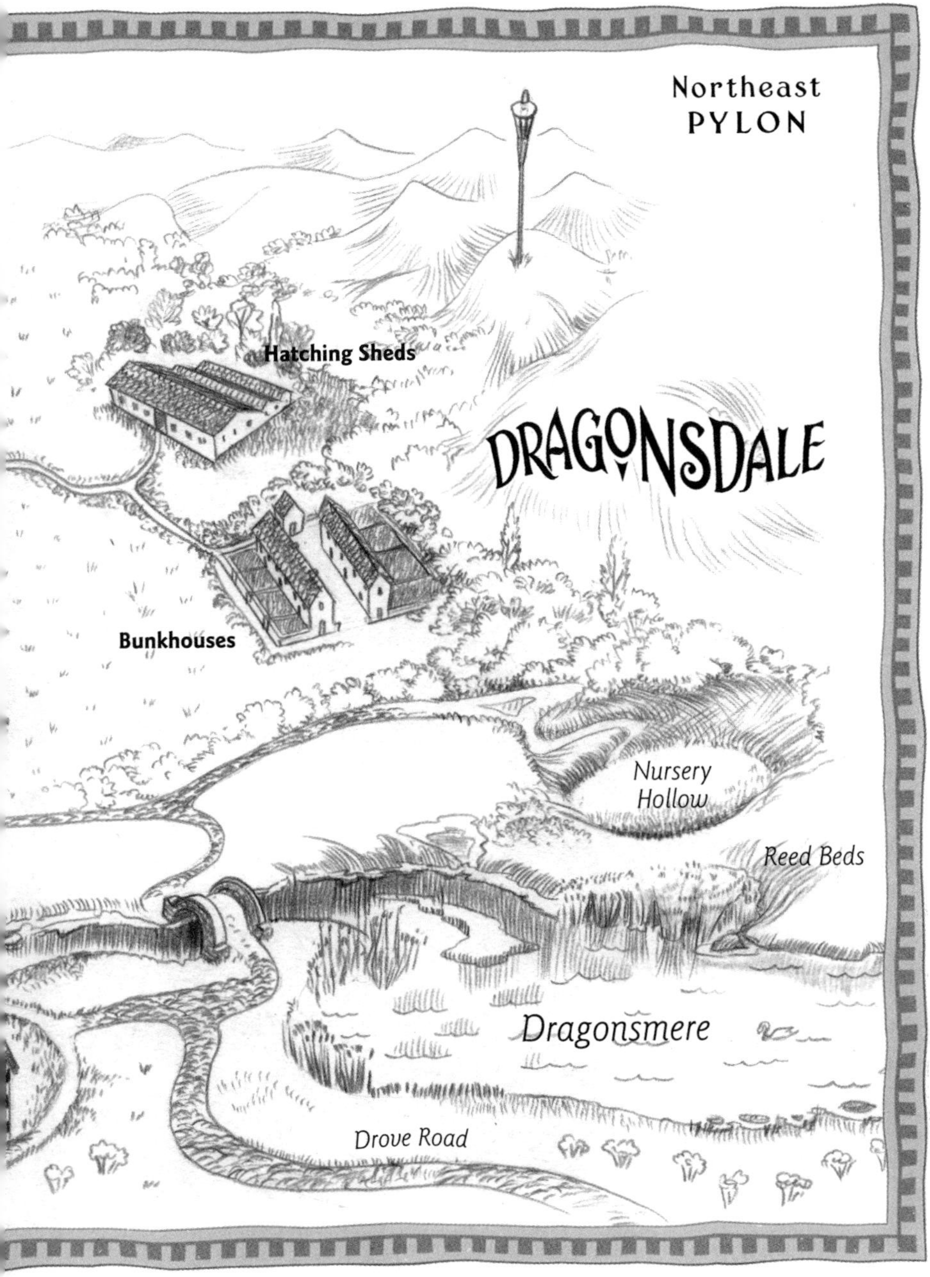

Northeast **PYLON**

Hatching Sheds

DRAGONSDALE

Bunkhouses

Nursery
Hollow

Reed Beds

Dragonsmere

Drove Road

The Isles of Bresal

Far out in the ocean, beyond all the shores we know,
hangs a huge bank of mist—the Veil.

The shimmering white curtain of the Veil
hides a wonderful secret.

For beyond the Veil lie the Isles of Bresal—
The Land of the Blessed.

The Isles are home to humans and merfolk, pards
and perytons, howlers and firedogs . . .

. . . and dragons.

For Ali

Text copyright © 2007 by Salamanda Drake
Illustrations copyright © 2007 by Gilly Marklew

First published in the United Kingdom in 2007
by Chicken House, 2 Palmer Street, Frome, Somerset BA11 1DS.
www.doublecluck.com

Library of Congress Cataloging-in-Publication Data Available

ISBN-13: 978-0-439-87173-0 • ISBN-10: 0-439-87173-5

10 9 8 7 6 5 4 3 2 1   07 08 09 10 11

Printed in China   62
First American edition, May 2007

The text type was set in Goudy Old Style.
The display type was set in Blackfriar.
Book design by Leyah Jensen

CONTENTS

MUCKING OUT

"**G**o away, Sky!"

Cara was exasperated. Skydancer's playful shove had knocked her halfway across the cobbled floor and made her drop her shovel. As she bent to pick it up, the dragon swung his head to give Cara another nudge. Cara turned around, raised the shovel, and tapped him briskly on the muzzle. Skydancer blinked and looked hurt.

"Don't go looking at me like that," said Cara. "How am I supposed to clean out your stall if you keep pushing me?"

Skydancer gave Cara one of his most pathetic looks. Cara laughed; Sky knew all her weak spots. She couldn't stay angry with him for long. She reached out and scratched the green scaly ridge between the golden blaze on the dragon's forehead and his left eye. Skydancer closed his great almond eyes and crooned with pleasure.

The dragon arched his back and stretched his forelegs so that his talons rose from the cobbles, falling back with a series of soft clicks as he relaxed. He half opened his wings, shaking his sails into new folds as his wing tips brushed the stable walls. Then he settled down again, twitching his long tail, the finlike spade at the end slapping the floor gently as Cara continued her affectionate stroking.

"I know you want to play." Cara tried hard to make her voice stern. "But I have to do my chores first. I've got to finish mucking out the other dragons' stables and check up on the dragonets. The longer you keep me here, the longer it'll take me to do them." Cara stopped scratching the dragon and straightened up. "I'll come back as soon as I can. I promise."

Sky gave a mournful chirrup and slunk over to his sleeping platform. He padded around in a circle a couple of times, like a huge scaly dog settling in its basket. Then he curled up with his nose tucked under his tail and gave Cara a self-pitying look.

Cara finished scooping up the smelly dragon droppings, waved good-bye to Skydancer, and stepped out of the dragon's stall into the stable yard. She dumped the mess into a wheelbarrow already piled high with the sweepings of other dragons' stalls and closed the heavy iron door behind her. Then she wiped her hands on her stained leather jerkin and brushed a wisp of dark reddish hair out of her eyes.

"Warm work!" Breena, who was cleaning out the stables on the other side of the yard, gave Cara a wave.

"And smelly!" Cara waved back.

"It's got to be done, though," said Breena. She

frowned and pursed her lips. In a fair imitation of Mistress Hildebrand, Dragonsdale's Chief Riding Instructor, she said, "Dragons aren't all fun and play, girls!" Cara giggled, and Breena gave her a knowing look. "Anyway, we can't afford to dillydally. Heaven help us if the whole place doesn't look spotless for the showing tomorrow."

Cara shuddered. "Don't remind me."

Breena looked surprised. "Aren't you looking forward to it? Wony's riding, isn't she?"

"If you can call it riding." Cara instantly regretted her snappishness. "Oh, I don't mean that. Poor Wony—she does her best, and she loves that little dragon of hers to bits . . ."

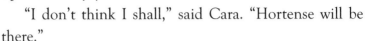

". . . but she does fall off quite a lot," finished Breena with a grin. "Cheer up. You'll enjoy it."

"I don't think I shall," said Cara. "Hortense will be there."

"Ah, Her Ladyship," said Breena knowingly. She shrugged. "Well, there's nothing you or I can do about Hortense. Just give her your very best smile . . ."

"Smile at Hortense?" said Cara in tones of deep disgust.

". . . and hope she falls off her dragon and lands in something smelly."

Cara grinned. "Now *that* I would enjoy. See you at lunch." Breena waved and stepped back into a stall.

Cara lifted the handles of the wheelbarrow. Her back gave a twinge, and she winced and set the barrow down again. She had been working hard since daybreak.

The sound of beating wings made her glance skyward: A formation of five dragons was flying overhead. Cara could just make out the shouts and calls of the riders as they urged their mounts into a perfect diamond pattern. She recognized Tord leading on Dawnspinner, his great Ridgeback Charger. Flying wing tip to wing tip, the guard wing turned over the white stone bulk of Dragonsdale House and headed out to patrol the wild lands that lay between Dragonsdale and the snowcapped peak of Cloudside, the tallest mountain on the Isle of Seahaven.

Cara trembled with a familiar, hot feeling of envy and longing. Since her earliest childhood, she had wanted to ride a dragon, to feel the rush of air as she flew, cradled between the sinuous neck and powerful shoulders, rocked by the beat of

the great wings. Yet all her life, she had helped raise dragons for others to ride. Why couldn't she be up there, in the blue sky and the wild wind, flying her own dragon, rather than stuck here mucking out the stables of Dragonsdale? If only she were allowed to ride . . .

"Woolgathering again?"

Cara started guiltily, and turned to face her father. "I only stopped for a moment, Da."

"I daresay." Huw the Dragonmaster was a stocky man, quite different in build from his slim, long-legged daughter. He had a snub nose and sharp gray eyes that missed nothing. Even in his sweat-stained tunic and shapeless riding breeches, the Dragonmaster's air of experience and authority made him an impressive figure. Huw was known throughout Bresal as owner and master of Dragonsdale, the most famous dragon-training farm in the whole of the Islands.

Cara's father jerked his grizzled head toward the door of Skydancer's stall. "I suppose you've been wasting time with that favorite of yours again."

"Sky has to be cleaned out," said Cara. "Just like all the others."

"I notice you take longer to clean him out than you do any of the rest."

Cara had no answer to this because it was true. "He gets so lonely."

This was a mistake. Her father frowned. "He wouldn't

get lonely if he allowed himself to be trained and ridden. Then he'd earn his keep like the rest. Dragonsdale is a training farm, not a rest home for idle dragons. We need guard dragons to protect us, hunting dragons to feed us, racing and show dragons to win competitions— if Skydancer keeps on defying his trainers . . ."

"But, Da," protested Cara, "Sky's a Goldenbrow—that's a very rare breed . . ."

"He could be as rare as a mermaid's toenails and he'd still be of no value to me if he won't allow himself to be trained. We can't afford to keep on stuffing food into useless mouths, that's all."

A cold hand seemed to clutch at Cara's heart. "Da?" She had asked the question many times before and knew it was hopeless, but she plowed on. "Why won't you let me ride Sky? I know I can do it! I know I can train him! Please . . ."

Cara broke off. Her father's face had darkened like a gathering storm. He didn't raise his voice, but his words lashed at Cara. "You know very well that I will not have you ride any dragon. You know why. We will not speak of this again. Is that clear?"

Cara hung her head.

The Dragonmaster glared at his daughter for a second or two longer, then nodded grimly. "Very well. Now, I have another job for you." Cara glanced up as her father put his fingers to his lips, gave a piercing whistle, and beckoned urgently. A small figure stepped out of the shadows at the far end of the stable yard and scurried to the Dragonmaster's side.

"This is Drane," said Huw. "He's from a farm up on the Walds. His father has asked me to take him on as apprentice stable lad." The Dragonmaster's expression said clearly that he had no great hopes for his new apprentice. Before Cara could say a "how-goes-your-day?" her father continued. "He can help you with your yard duties. Show him the ropes, and take him up to the house for lunch when you've finished—as long as the dragons haven't eaten him by then." A look of horror crossed Drane's face, and he gulped. "And don't dawdle," added Huw brusquely. "You know Dragonsdale will be on show tomorrow. No one wants to buy a dragon from a stable that looks like a pigsty." He turned on his heel and strode off.

Cara studied her new assistant. Drane was a thin-faced boy with untidy, mousy hair. He was wearing a woolen jerkin and a woebegone expression.

Cara wrinkled her nose. "Is that all you've got to wear?" Drane nodded glumly. "We'll have to find you some leathers," Cara told him. "Wool won't last five minutes around dragons."

Drane looked nervously toward the stalls. "W-why?"

"You'll find out." Cara was a kindhearted girl, but the argument with her father—the latest of many—had made her bad-tempered. She wasn't pleased about having to play nursemaid to an apprentice. He would probably turn out to be completely useless, anyway. In Cara's view, most boys were; certainly the ones who started work at the stables didn't seem to last long. "Come on."

Cara wheeled her barrow to the next stall in line. She peered in through the narrow top doorway before sliding the iron bolt across to open the heavy bottom door. Turning, she saw that Drane had not followed her. The new apprentice stable lad was hanging back, a terrified expression on his face. Cara stared at him. "Have you done much work with dragons before?"

Drane shook his head.

"Then why do you want to work here?"

"I don't," Drane burst out. "It was my father's idea."

Oh, great, thought Cara. Aloud, she said, "Are you scared of dragons?"

Drane looked down and shuffled his feet. Reluctantly, he nodded. "A bit."

Cara groaned. This was just getting better and better. "Well, you'll have to start somewhere. Come over here." Drane took a step back. "Come on!"

Feet dragging, Drane shuffled forward.

Cara opened the door to the stall. "This is Breezeskimmer," she said briskly. "You can see her name on the brass plate over the door." Drane looked up, read the plate (his lips moved, Cara couldn't help noticing), and nodded glumly. "She's a Silvertip, a racing dragon."

Drane's brow furrowed. "Racing dragon?"

"Yes. There are lots of different types of dragon, surely you must know that?"

Drane shook his head, and Cara pursed her lips at this display of willful ignorance. She held out her hand, folding a finger against her palm as she named each dragon type. "Well, at Dragonsdale we have guard dragons—they're the biggest—and hunting dragons. Then we have show dragons—and racing dragons, like Breezy here. She should be out exercising with the others, but she's had a bad dose of colic. Alberich Dragonleech has been to see her—"

"Who?"

Cara tried to find the words that would explain the baffling new world of the stables in a way that Drane would understand. "A surgeon looks after sick humans," she said eventually, "and a dragonleech looks after sick dragons. Alberich is the best in the Islands. Anyway, he treated Breezy and now we're dosing her with flax oil and keeping her in for a couple of days until she's feeling better. Hi, Breezy!"

Shouldering her shovel, Cara marched into the stall and began to scoop. Drane poked his head fearfully around the door and stared.

Silvertips weren't among the larger breeds of dragons, but to Drane, Breezeskimmer looked enormous. The boy flinched as the dragon shifted uncomfortably on her sleeping platform and gave a hiccup. A thin, bluish flame dribbled from the corner of her mouth.

Cara looked up. "Come on in! Don't be shy."

Drane edged into the stall, looking ready to bolt. "She won't eat me, will she?"

Cara stopped scooping and stared at him. "Why would she do that?"

"The Dragonmaster said I might get eaten."

"He was joking."

"Oh," said Drane miserably. "Ha-ha."

"Dragons don't eat people," said Cara. "Not anymore. Savage creatures like pards eat people, and so do firedogs and howlers, given half the chance. You're a lot safer in here than you would be out in the hills."

Drane gave a bitter smile. "Or even back on the farm."

"Oh, your farm should be pretty safe with Dragonsdale to protect you."

Drane's expression was suddenly cold and withdrawn. "Not Dragonsdale," he said. "We were bound to Clapperclaw."

Cara pursed her lips at the mention of the rival stable. "Even so . . ." Her voice trailed off. She could tell that she had touched upon a sore point with Drane, but she had no idea what she had said to upset him, or how to put it right. After an uncomfortable silence, she said, "Well, anyway, this is a dragon's stable."

Drane looked around dubiously. "It's not like the barns we had back on the farm. They had walls made of wood and a thatched roof."

Cara gave him an amused look. "Fine for docile, hairy

farm beasts—but dragons breathe fire, remember." She pointed. "The walls are stone. The beams for the roof are made of bog oak, which is practically flameproof, and the roof is made of clay tile. The doors are iron, see? A wide bottom door for getting in and out, and a narrow top door to let light in."

Drane eyed the grunting dragon. "She doesn't look very comfortable. Our animals get straw to lie on."

Cara laughed. "Yes, but these are dragons! It's not much good having a bed you might set fire to every time you sneeze! The sleeping platforms are made of pumice."

"Isn't that a rock?"

"Well, yes, but as rocks go, it's pretty soft. Anyway, Breezy isn't uncomfortable because her bed's too hard. She's uncomfortable because she's got a tummy ache, isn't that right, Breezy?" The dragon hooted miserably. "Go and scratch her eye ridges," Cara told Drane. "All dragons like that. It'll make her feel better."

Hesitantly, Drane inched closer to the dragon and reached out. His fingers brushed the ridges above Breezeskimmer's lustrous yellow eyes.

"Harder," Cara told him. "She's a dragon. You won't hurt her."

"I wasn't worried about me hurting her," said Drane, but he scratched harder. Immediately, the dragon's eyes closed and she began to make a rumbling sound in her chest.

Cara swept the droppings out through the doorway. "Good, only two more stalls to do."

Drane was still scratching. "I think she likes me. She's purring."

"She's doing what?"

"Purring."

Cara shook her head. "Dragons don't purr . . . uh-oh." She beckoned to Drane. "I think you'd better come out of there."

"Why?" Drane's voice was dreamy. "She's enjoying it. Look, she's smiling."

"Drane, I think it would be a really good idea if you came out of there right now."

Drane shuffled over to the door. "I don't see what all the rush is for . . . aaargh!" he concluded as Cara dragged him out by the front of his jerkin. She slammed the bottom door and dropped to her knees.

Breezeskimmer shifted unhappily on her sleeping platform. The buildup of gas in her second stomach was making the dragon feel very uncomfortable indeed. She hooted a warning to the human boy, who was still peering over the top of the door to her stall. Breezeskimmer had been trained never to breathe fire when there was a human being in the way, but this time she couldn't help it.

The dragon gave a gigantic belch. A searing tongue of flame shot from her mouth across the stall and roared toward the open doorway, straight for Drane's unprotected head.

HATCHLINGS
AND WYVERNS

Cara crouched in the shelter of the solid iron door. Above her, Breezeskimmer's flame leapt, hissing, crackling, and writhing almost as if it were alive. It washed against the stones of the well that stood in the middle of the stable yard.

The flame died as suddenly as it had erupted. Cara stood up, brushing muck off her knees, and peered into Breezeskimmer's stall. "That's better, isn't it, Breezy? You're looking a lot happier—" She broke off as she realized that Drane was still crouched on the soiled cobbles of the stable yard. He had his hands over his ears and was gibbering with terror. "What's the matter with you?"

"You said she w-w-wouldn't eat me!"

"Well, she didn't."

"But she n-n-nearly b-b-burned my head off!"

"Yes, but she didn't mean to," said Cara cheerfully. "It was your own fault for getting in the way." Drane gawped at her. "In any case, I pulled you out of there in time, didn't I? Nothing to make a fuss about."

On the other side of the yard, Breena peered over the door of a stall and clicked her tongue. "Breezy!" she said. "Where are your manners?"

Cara grinned back. "Better out than in." She turned back to Drane. "Well, come on. You can help me clean out the next stall."

Drane sat down rather suddenly on the pile of droppings that Cara had just shoveled out of Breezeskimmer's stall. "Actually, I feel a bit faint. I think I'll just sit here for a time and wait until you've finished."

"Please yourself, but I wouldn't sit there for too long." Cara raised an eyebrow.

Drane looked down and realized what he was sitting in. "Awww . . ."

Cara took pity on him. "Never mind, I'll do the stall myself—it's the last one, anyway."

Ten minutes later, she dumped her wheelbarrow load carefully onto the gently steaming dung heap at the back of the stables. She parked the barrow in the lean-to shelter at the end of the yard and beckoned to Drane. "One more job before lunch."

Drane's face was haggard. "More dragons?"

"Yes, but only little ones."

Cara led the way from the stables. In the distant practice area, young dragons and their riders were preparing for the next day's showing, flying through and between obstacles suspended from towering masts, while on both sides of the valley, above the rolling meadows surrounding Dragonsdale, the more experienced riders rehearsed aerobatic maneuvers—swooping and spinning, looping and rolling, making tight turns around the four great pylons that marked the flying area above the training farm.

After a brief envious glance at the soaring dragons, Cara kept her eyes firmly on the path ahead. She didn't want to watch others having a good time, perfecting their dragonriding skills, doing all the things she was forbidden to do herself.

Two small figures were trudging across the meadow from the direction of the nursery hollow, making for the stable yard. One was a plump girl with short blond hair, the other a diminutive dragon with an untidy crest, a barrel-shaped body, and stumpy legs and wings.

Cara took in the girl's rumpled appearance and shook her head in exasperation. "Oh, Wony! Don't tell me you fell off Bumble again."

The little dragon hung his head in embarrassment. Wony knuckled her eyes, trying not to cry. "Yes, Cara. I forgot to do up my saddle belt again." Wony blinked at Cara's exasperated expression. "And I got tipped out, and Bumble couldn't fly properly with me dangling on the tether, so he dragged me through a hedge and then we landed in a heap. It wasn't Bumble's fault. Mistress Hildebrand says he gets tired easily; he needs to exercise his wings." Bumble fluttered his wings in mournful agreement.

"Don't worry." Cara gave the unhappy girl a quick hug. "At least you're early for lunch. Go to the feed store and find Bumble a nice fresh brace of coneys to keep his strength up."

Wony brightened. "Oh, yes—and then I can go to the kitchen and get some cake—to keep *my* strength up."

Cara laughed. "All right—but make sure you feed Bumble first."

"Yes, Cara." Wony and her dragon hurried away, and Cara looked down the gentle slope toward the nursery hollow. This was the lowest part of the farm. To avoid accidents, warning pylons surrounded the area where the three-year-old dragons and their young riders were practicing their basic flying skills. From her high wooden platform overlooking the hollow, Mistress Hildebrand's strident voice drifted faintly on the breeze as she put the youngsters through their paces. "Posture, Lavinia! Think straight back! Adelheid! What are you doing with those reins? Hands! Hands! Good grief, girl, you're supposed to be a dragonrider, not a sack of turnips. . . ."

Cara smiled sadly. Even youngsters half her age got to ride a dragon. She shook her head and led the way to the hatchling sheds. Drane trudged along behind.

"Don't dawdle," Cara told him. "There's still a lot to do before the showing tomorrow."

Drane quickened his pace. "The Dragonmaster said something about Dragonsdale being on show," he said. "Is that what he meant?"

Cara nodded. "It's only a local event really, but it's a qualifier for the Island Championships, so there'll be a fair crowd. It's important that our dragons do well in the competitions—then people will know that my father's a good trainer and they'll want to send their dragons to us. The dragons we're breeding will become more valuable, too." She pulled open the sliding door of the hatchling sheds, slipped through, and waited for Drane to join her. She closed the door before adding, "And Lord Torin will be there."

"Will he?" said Drane woodenly. "That'll be nice."

Cara gave the new apprentice a sideways glance. "He wouldn't bother, what with him being High Lord of the Island and all that, but his daughter is riding. So thanks to Hortense"—she grimaced, as though speaking this name had left a nasty taste in her mouth—"it's even more important that we're all in our smartest clothes and on our best behavior." She sniffed. "Anyway, there's plenty of time to worry about all that after lunch. We've got a job to do here first."

The hatchling sheds were a labyrinth of nesting pens, where dragon eggs were hatched and young dragons reared. Cara led Drane into the midst of the gloomy interior and pointed to a large pen. "In there."

Drane peered into the pen. It was occupied by around a dozen dragonets, as big as the pigs he had tended back on his farm. The young dragons were miniature versions of the full-grown ones, except that they were much chubbier and their wings were even more stubby than Bumble's. Some were playing in the sand, while others were lying higgledy-piggledy on top of one another, snoring, with their legs in the air and their muzzles twitching. "They

look like puppies," said Drane. "Why do you keep them all together like that?"

"They like one another's company when they're young."

Cara busied herself with a piece of equipment that looked like an overgrown set of scales.

"What's that?" asked Drane.

"It's a weighing machine." Cara pointed at the dragonets. "We have to weigh them." She finished adjusting the balance. "You catch them, give them to me, and I'll weigh them."

"Catch them?" Drane was aghast. "Won't they fly away?"

"They can't fly at this age."

"They'll burn me!"

"They can't flame at this age, either. You can start with that one."

The next few minutes were very exciting. Several times, Drane disappeared completely under a swarm of overexcited dragonets. Occasionally he managed to catch one, but the supple little creature usually managed to squirm out of his hands before he could get it to Cara. Sometimes he brought her the same dragonet twice.

The little dragons couldn't fly, but they could certainly jump, whirring their tiny wings like startled chickens. Eventually, a rocketing dragonet hit Drane headfirst in the stomach, and he sat down with a "Whoof!"

"I've got an idea," said Cara. "I'll catch them, and you weigh them."

This was a little better, but not much. The dragonets wriggled out of Drane's grasp before they could be weighed, and Cara had to chase them all around the shed.

"I've got an even better idea," said Cara eventually. "I'll catch them and I'll weigh them."

"And what shall I do?"

"You stand over there and stay out of the way."

Weighing the hatchlings, and recording the weights in the breeding ledger, took so long that by the time Cara and Drane had made their way back past the stables to Dragonsdale House, they were late for lunch. Cara opened the kitchen door. Smells of cooking wafted out, making her mouth water. She stepped into the warmth.

Sitting at an enormous oak table were an assorted group of stable hands and riders dressed for flying in thick leather boots, breeches, and jerkins. One or two of them looked up and gave Cara a nod and a grunt of welcome. Then Drane appeared. Instantly there was an explosion of hissing, a flutter of batlike wings—and two wyverns launched themselves from the mantelshelf, where they had been basking in the heat of the huge black kitchen range, on which pots and kettles boiled and bubbled. The angry little creatures flew at Drane, pecking and clutching at his hair with their sharp talons. Drane fell to his knees and tried to protect his head with his hands.

Cara shooed the indignant wyverns away. "Leave him alone!" she cried. "This is Drane—he's new."

An older rider with a gaunt, weather-beaten face and a grizzled beard helped Drane up. "Sorry about that," he said, "they're not used to strangers. You'll find they're really friendly when they get to know you."

Still hissing at Drane and giving him malevolent glances, the wyverns settled back on their perches. Drane eyed them warily. "I'll look forward to that."

The rider's mouth twitched. Then he turned back to the table. "Eat up. Tord's patrol will be back soon, and it'll be our turn. We've had reports of firedogs and howlers sniffing around one or two of the local farms, and there are rumors of pards up in the hills, so stay alert." He pointed an accusing finger at one of the younger riders. "No sneaking off to chase perytons, all right?" The rider flushed, while his colleagues winked and nudged one another. "Those things may be good eating," the older rider went on, "but they fly like the wind, and we've no time to spare for hunting. Let's go." He marched out. The other riders hastily drained their bowls and followed him, those who had not finished their meal surreptitiously tucking hunks of bread into their jerkins on the way.

As the door slammed behind them, Drane turned to Cara. "Firedogs and howlers—what's he going to do about them?"

"That's Galen," Cara told him. "He's our Chief Huntsman and he leads the guard flight."

Drane looked unimpressed. He pointed at the wyverns. "What are those monsters, anyway? Baby dragons?"

Cara shook her head. "Wyverns. Dragons have four legs. Wyverns only have two, see? They keep the mice down." She turned to the roly-poly, ruddy-faced woman who had just come bustling up the cellar steps and was now busily lifting pans from the range. "Hello, Gerda. What's for lunch?"

"You're late." The woman shook a large wooden spoon at the new arrivals. "I've told you about being late, Cara. There's no lamb stew and dumplings left. Galen and his gannets have just had the last of it."

Cara gave a sigh. "Sorry. I had to look after Drane here."

Gerda looked Drane up and down. "And I suppose you'll be expecting food as well. . . ."

Drane glanced at Cara, not knowing what to say.

The housekeeper grinned, tapped her nose, and gave Cara an exaggerated wink. "No lamb stew, but it just so happens that I've got some freshly baked bread, vegetable soup, and a large chunk of somebody's favorite cheese, newly churned and set!"

Cara clapped her hands in delight. "Thank you, Gerda! How would I do without you?"

"Very badly!" said Gerda sternly. "Both you and your father." But then the housekeeper's face creased into a huge smile, and she burst into a bellow of raucous laughter. Everything about Gerda was larger than life, and Cara loved her for it.

The promised meal was laid out, and Drane and Cara eagerly set about the food as the hands left to continue their chores.

Cara finished quickly, and heartlessly left Drane to help Gerda with the washing-up while she slipped out to the stables to snatch a few minutes with Sky. As she stroked and groomed the dragon, she told him all about her morning with Drane. "You should have seen him trying to catch the dragonets!" Cara did a spirited pantomime of Drane chasing the little dragons, clucking as though he were trying to round up chickens. Sky gave a draconic warble. "He's all right for a boy," Cara admitted, "but talk about two left hands! He's pretty hopeless really."

"Who is?" Drane asked suspiciously, peering over the stable door.

Cara gave him a bright smile. "Oh, just someone I know. Gerda didn't keep you for long."

Drane flushed. "I broke a plate, and she said I could go. Actually, she was quite insistent about it." Cara laughed.

Drane went on. "Then I met your friend Breena—she told me you'd be here. She says she's a bit pushed for time and could you help her with Moonflight?"

Guiltily, Cara said good-bye to Sky, who thrust his head over the bottom door of his stable as Cara closed it behind her, and hooted plaintively as she hurried across the stable yard to help her friend. On the way, she peered into Bumble's stall. Wony, with her tongue sticking out in concentration, was busily choosing brightly colored strips of green ribbon and tying them through the pierced scales of her dragon's crest. Cara clicked her tongue and shook her head in exasperation. "Wony, you know that's a waste of time. Those ribbons will get filthy before tomorrow, and you'll only have to do the job all over again."

Wony's face fell. "But Bumble likes having his crest tied—and they look so pretty," she added wistfully.

"I daresay," said Cara severely. "But he likes having his scales polished as well, and that's what you should be doing right now."

"Yes, Cara." With a sigh, Wony relinquished her ribbons and picked up a scraper.

"Cleaning a dragon's scales is hard work," Cara told Drane as they made their way across the yard. "That's why Wony would keep putting it off if I let her. But it's got to be done. Dirt under the scales makes a dragon uncomfortable. Anyway, it's a vital part of the Trustbond." Seeing Drane's blank look, Cara explained. "Cleaning and grooming help to establish trust between dragons and their riders."

"You mean cleaning dragons makes them tame?"

Cara shook her head firmly. "Dragons aren't tame. They're wild creatures. Never forget that. But they allow us to ride them because of the Trustbond. Hi, Breena!"

Moonflight, Breena's dragon, hooted a welcome. Breena looked up, flushed from her efforts. She brushed a few strands of straggling hair behind her ear. "Hi, Cara. Come to lend a hand?"

"That's what I'm here for. What would you like me to do?"

"Could you oil Moony's wings?" Breena pointed a hooked scraping tool at her dragon's flank. "I'm having to dig the dirt out from every scale. She likes rolling in the mud, which is all very well, but guess who has to do the cleanup?" Moonflight craned her long, flexible neck to gaze adoringly at her mistress. "Yes, you I'm talking about, you great mucky thing!" The dragon nuzzled her rider's neck. "Oh, get on with you." Breena went back to work.

Cara collected a soft cloth and a bottle of grooming oil from the cleaning materials Breena had brought. Drane hovered uncertainly. "What can I do?"

"You can polish her claws," said Cara.

Drane eyed the dragon's long, razor-sharp, curved claws without enthusiasm. "I'd really rather not."

Cara grinned at him. "All right—in that case you can clean her tack. There's wax in the pot over there." She handed Drane a cloth. "Put plenty on and rub it well in—it keeps the leather supple. Start with the head harness."

Drane turned the harness over awkwardly, unsure of where to begin. Cara ignored him and held up the bottle of oil and cloth for Moonflight's inspection. The dragon grunted and obligingly spread one great wing with a graceful movement typical of the Darkeye breed. Cara poured oil onto the cloth and reached up, noticing as she did so that Drane had somehow managed to get his head between the cheekpieces of the harness, with the browband caught awkwardly under one shoulder. Taking no notice of his struggles, Cara set to her task, working methodically at oiling Moonflight's sails from the front of the wing to the trailing edge. The dragon crooned with pleasure as the cooling oil spread over her wing membranes.

"Help!"

Cara turned to find that Drane had now managed to get himself hopelessly tangled in the leather straps he was supposed to be polishing. She rolled her eyes and went to his rescue. "How in the Islands did you manage to get the muzzle-band around your neck?" she demanded, tugging at straps and buckles.

"I don't know, it just—ow!—sort of worked its way up there. . . ."

"I hope I'm not interrupting anything." The cool, insinuating voice came from the stable door.

Cara turned. A tall, fair girl wearing a spotless riding habit was standing in the open doorway, watching her struggles to separate Drane from the wayward harness with an expression that balanced condescension with spite.

Cara straightened up and faced the newcomer, taking great care to keep her voice level and her face expressionless.

"Hello, Hortense."

DANGER IN
THE NIGHT

"Don't mind me," drawled Hortense. "Please, don't stop—whatever it was you were doing."

Cara seethed inwardly. Trust Drane to put her in an embarrassing situation—and trust Hortense to make the most of it. But she only said, "What do you want?"

Hortense turned to indicate the mournful-looking dragon she was leading. "I want you to get Cloudbreaker ready for Best Presented at tomorrow's showing."

Cara's eyes narrowed. "Oh, you do, do you?"

"Yes," drawled Hortense. "Why not? After all, it's not as if you've got a dragon of your own to groom, is it?"

Cara clenched her fists and took a step forward.

She felt a light touch on her arm, and Breena appeared at her side, rubbing her hands on a cloth. "Prepare your dragon, Hortense?" she said mildly. "All competitors are supposed to groom their own dragons, you know that."

Hortense eyed Cloudbreaker with contempt. "In the first place, this fat lazy lump isn't my dragon—he belongs to Dragonsdale, so I don't see why I should scrub his grubby hide." The dragon gave Hortense a cold, reptilian stare, which she ignored. "And in the second place, I've far more important things to do with my time. Anyway, Breena, you've got Cara helping you get your dragon ready."

"Cara is kindly working as a stable hand under my supervision," Breena told her stiffly. "That's allowed."

"Well, then, she can work as a stable hand under my supervision."

"And where will you be supervising her from? A nice, comfortable couch up at your father's manor?"

"Oh, I'm sure I can trust Cara to do a good job." Hortense gave Cara a nasty smile. "After all, she wouldn't like everyone to say that her father's precious stables had provided Lord Torin's daughter with a badly turned-out dragon . . . would you, Cara?"

Cara didn't trust herself to speak. Without a word, she took Cloudbreaker's head reins and murmured endearments to the disconsolate dragon. Hortense gave her a triumphant sneer and stalked away.

Breena watched the departing figure, a dangerous glint in her eye. "One of these days . . ."

"Never mind." Cara patted Cloudbreaker on the cheek. "I wouldn't want her grooming poor old Cloudy, anyway. She'd probably give him scale rot. It's bad enough being *ridden* by her, isn't it, boy?" Cloudbreaker gave a hoot of agreement.

Breena was still seething. "It's just not fair. That no-good, work-shy, stuck-up good-for-nothing will be riding tomorrow, while you . . ." Seeing Cara's desolate expression, she broke off abruptly. "Sorry."

"It's all right," said Cara.

"Well, it isn't, so."

Cara sighed and patted Cloudbreaker's neck. "Come on, boy, let's get you cleaned up." She gave Breena an apologetic look. "'Fraid I'll have to leave Moonflight to you, but you can have Drane. He'll be some help."

"I don't think so." Breena directed a critical look over her shoulder into the stable where Drane was struggling in a leathery spiderweb of his own making. "He seems to have got himself tied up in the reins now."

Grooming Cloudbreaker was no easy task. Cara cursed Hortense under her breath as she struggled to make the unhappy dragon presentable. Lord Torin's daughter was not only proud and haughty, and scornful of anyone she regarded as a social inferior (which was practically everybody), but she neglected her dragons shamefully.

All the Dragonsdale riders, and those who lived elsewhere but kept their dragons at the stables, took care of their own mounts. Even the riders who hired dragons from Huw would be expected to make sure their dragon was properly fed and groomed after every flight. But Hortense, on alighting from the saddle, would simply throw the reins to whomever happened to be about in the yard and disappear. Huw would not have tolerated such failure of care from any other rider; however, Hortense was Lord Torin's daughter, and the Dragonmaster could not afford to offend the High Lord of Seahaven.

Dragonsdale stable hands were always busy, and while not one of them would intentionally neglect a dragon, they had no time to do a lazy rider's work in addition to their own. In any case, nobody wanted to put themselves out for Hortense's benefit. The result was that Cloudbreaker, though not uncared-for, was certainly not in anything like the condition required for a showing.

Hortense never rode any dragon for long. Usually, after a few flights had exposed her many failings, she would start to complain that these shortcomings were really her dragon's fault. For although what few skills she possessed had been learned at Dragonsdale, Hortense was a terrible rider. Mistress Hildebrand had resigned three times because the Dragonmaster had refused to throw Hortense out of her classes, but in the end the Chief Riding Instructor had always swallowed her pride and come back.

A good rider learned to guide a dragon, kindly but firmly. Hortense's idea of riding a dragon was to use force at all times. After a few weeks of this treatment, Huw would insist on a change of mount so that no dragon had to suffer Hortense for longer than necessary. However, Hortense would have to turn in a halfway decent performance to qualify for the Island Championships, so she had been partnered with Cloudbreaker for some time now, and it showed.

The problem wasn't only that the dragon's wings were dry, his claws and horns chipped and dull, and his scales lusterless. What made matters worse was that being ridden by Hortense had made Cloudbreaker bad-tempered, mistrustful, and thoroughly fed up with humans in general. He was in no mood to be cooperative. The cleaning process made him itch, and he snapped at Cara several times when the blade of her scraper slipped between the scales to touch a tender spot. Nor was he pleased when the vinegar she was using to polish his scales trickled into a scratch or graze.

He only mellowed when Cara rubbed soothing oil into his wing sails, and by the time she came to file and polish his horns and claws, he had become quite biddable. But by that time, the light had faded from the sky, and Cara had to finish her task by the light of a lantern. She was exhausted, and much as she liked Cloudbreaker, she was very relieved to pack away the cleaning materials and slip the bolt on his stall. She looked in on Sky, but the dragon was asleep, curled up on his pumice bed with his tail tucked under his nose and his legs twitching as he chased perytons in his dreams. Cara didn't have the heart to wake him.

It was late by the time she left the stables, and the yard was deserted except for the watch dragon, which flapped its clipped wings and hooted a challenge. Cara reassured it, and called a "good night" to the lookout on the balcony of the stone bell tower that rose from the northeast corner of the yard. The muffled figure waved back and resumed his watch for any danger that might come from the hills to threaten Dragonsdale.

On entering the house, Cara was not surprised to find that she had missed supper. She went straight to bed and lay fully dressed on the coverlet, aching in every joint. It took her a long time to get to sleep.

Cara was jerked wide awake by the clamor of the alarm bell yelling and hammering through the sleeping house. She scrambled out of bed and flung open the curtains. Torches were already flaring in the yard, the watch dragon's frantic summons was being taken up by every beast in the stables, and up in the hills, beacons blazed. One of the local farms was being raided. The Dragonsdale guard flight was being summoned to help.

Cara struggled into her clothes and raced from the room. All around her, muffled thumps, curses, and hurrying footsteps echoed through the house as hands and riders turned out of bed and stumbled, still half asleep, to their posts.

The stable yard was crowded as Cara emerged from the house. Huw was barking orders at stable hands while Galen marshalled the guard wings. Breena was leading Galen's dragon, Nightrider, from the stable. She jerked her head at Cara, who nodded and raced to the tack

<caption>DRAGONSDALE</caption>

room to collect Nightrider's harness. Working with deft, practiced movements, she and Breena saddled the great Ridgeback Charger while Galen briefed his riders.

"The call is from Thorngarth. We don't know the nature of the threat, so be careful. I'll take my wing in to see what we're dealing with; Tord and Imar, your wings will circle to the south and wait for instructions. Understood?"

The riders, buckling helmets, adjusting scarves, and pulling on goggles and leather gauntlets, nodded. Galen glanced around to see that the dragons were fully harnessed and ready to go. "Where's Mellan?"

Imar, the leader of Mellan's wing, frowned. "Injured in training this morning, Galen."

"Young fool," said the guard leader without heat. "Well, I daresay we'll manage without him."

Breena stepped forward. "Let me take Mellan's place, Galen. I've done practice flights with the guard wings, and I can have Moonflight harnessed in two wingbeats."

Galen gave the eager girl a glance of tolerant amusement. "Only senior riders fly guard, Breena. You know that. In any case, we can't wait." He turned away from Breena's furious glare, raised his arm, and made a clenched fist. "Move out."

The riders mounted and took the reins from the attendant stable hands. Dragons headed out of the yard in flight order. One by one, they launched themselves into the night sky to wheel above Dragonsdale, barely visible in the flickering torchlight from below. As each wing formed, it soared away into the darkness and disappeared.

Breena glowered after the departing dragons. "Galen is such a . . . a male! He knows I'm good enough to join the guard, and Moony could outfly most of those lumbering beasts with both her wings in splints."

"That may be so." Breena winced as a deep voice sounded right behind her. She turned to face the Dragonmaster's scowl. "Moonflight is a fine beast," Huw continued. "She was, after all, raised at Dragonsdale. But you have yet to prove yourself. For all your skill, you are not yet a senior rider. Nor are you experienced in night flying, to say nothing of dealing with dangerous predators. We'll see whether you qualify for the Island Championships before we start talking about guard duty." Huw stumped away to join the stream of stable hands heading for the kitchen to take refuge from the raw night air and drink steaming mugs of hot soup. Breena watched him go, with folded arms and a face like thunder.

"Maybe it's just as well you're not going," Cara told her. "Just think—if you had flown guard tonight, all the work you did on Moonflight for the showing would be spoiled. You'd have to start all over again." Breena remained unmollified. "And at least you'll have the chance of flying guard one day," said Cara wistfully. "That's more than some of us will ever get."

Breena thawed immediately. "I suppose so." She gave

Cara a guilty look. "And I'm sorry I couldn't come and give you a hand after I'd finished. I got nabbed by Gerda to help out with preparations for the showing. She had us making enough cakes, pies, and tarts to feed the whole of Seahaven."

Cara laughed. "That's Gerda all over. . . ."

She broke off as Drane appeared, blinking sleepily in the torchlight. His jerkin was laced askew and his hair looked like a badly weathered bird's nest.

"Good afternoon, Drane!" said Breena acidly. "Nice of you to join us when all the work's been done."

Drane was too befuddled to notice her sarcasm. "What's happening? What have I missed?"

"There's been an attack on one of our farms," Cara told him. "Thorngarth. They pay us a tithe for protection, and they've lit their beacon to summon our help. The guard wings have flown out to see what the matter is."

Drane gave a bark of mirthless laughter. "Have they? That's good of them."

Cara and Breena stared at him. "What's that supposed to mean?" demanded Breena.

"Oh, nothing important," said Drane bitterly. "It's just that when we called, no one came." He turned his back and mooched away back into the stable yard.

Breena and Cara exchanged glances. Then Cara hurried after Drane. "Wait!" Drane stopped but did not turn. Cara took him by the arm. "Drane—what do you mean? Your farm was bound to Clapperclaw, you said."

"We were," said Drane in a hard, flat voice. "But when a pack of firedogs attacked us last month, they didn't come."

Cara was aghast. "That's terrible! If your farm paid a tithe to Clapperclaw, they had a duty to help you. Didn't you complain to Lord Torin?"

"We tried. But my father was never exactly good at paying his tithes on time, and Dragonmaster Adair made some excuse about being overstretched. In any case, Torin found in their favor. We lost a third of our stock. It nearly ruined us. That's why I'm here—there were just too many mouths to feed at home."

Cara said nothing. She pressed Drane's arm in a gesture of sympathy. Getting no response, she turned away and crossed the yard to Skydancer's stall. Drane disappeared in the direction of the bunkhouse.

Like all the other dragons, Sky had been excited and disturbed by the alarm and the departure of the guard flight. Cara stroked his muzzle to soothe him.

"Poor Drane," she said. "No wonder he was quiet when I talked about farms being under our protection. And no wonder he doesn't think much of dragons." Skydancer gave a questioning chirrup. "Oh, not you, Sky. I'm sure he likes you. . . ."

Skydancer keened softly. The dragon was still staring out through the open upper door, at the point in the sky where the guard flight had vanished. "What is it, Sky?" asked Cara softly. "Are you remembering the night Galen and Nightrider found you out in the wilds?" She fell silent. Immediately after she said the words, Cara chided herself for being foolish and sentimental. Sky had been far too young to remember how, as a hatchling, he had been found crying over the dead body of his mother. The wild dragon had arrived back at her nest too late to stop a pride of pards from killing the rest of her brood. She had evidently died defending Sky, destroying many of the great spotted cats in her fury. When Galen and his dragon had arrived, the surviving pards had been circling the mother and her dragonet cautiously, not quite believing that the terrible creature who had slain their fellows was dead. But dead she was, and dead the young Skydancer would have been, had not Nightrider picked him up in his powerful talons and brought him to Dragonsdale.

Cara's hand was still. Sky honked indignantly and pushed his nose beneath it. "Sorry, Sky." Cara awoke from her reverie and resumed stroking. "I know how you feel. I know you want to be out there with the others. So do I. I'd love us to fly through the dark together with the moon above us and the land all mist and shadow below . . ." She sighed. "But it's not going to happen." The dragon gave a mournful hoot. Cara tweaked his ear. "Don't be sad. At least we're together—"

She broke off. Leaving Sky, who rumbled in protest, she tiptoed across the stable and peered through the half-open door, out into the yard. It was deserted now. Breena had either followed the others into the kitchen or gone to console Moonflight as Cara had Sky.

Cara carefully pulled the top door closed, then returned to Skydancer. She tapped the dragon on his shoulder, and Sky instantly raised his foreleg so that Cara could step up onto it. From there, she reached up for the dorsal scale at the nape of Sky's neck and hauled herself into the rider's position on the dragon's back. Sky made no protest.

Cara reached down to stroke the dragon's neck, feeling the muscles ripple beneath the scales as he lowered his foreleg. "Do you think about flying, Sky?" she said softly. "I do—all the time. The two of us, riding the wind, swooping and soaring in the cold air and all the world laid out before us . . ."

Cara remained there, whispering to Sky and caressing him, until at length her head nodded forward and she lay across Skydancer's neck as sleep overcame her. Slowly, a smile spread across her face. In her dreams Cara and her beloved dragon were no longer tied to the earth, stuck down in the clay, but soaring free, sweeping through the vault of the sky, while the land with all its duties and disappointments fell away below, and the Isles of Bresal dwindled until they were mere specks in the silver sea, imperfections in a mirror.

Cara was awoken by the clap of wing beats overhead, announcing the return of the guard flight. Sliding quickly from Sky's back, her throat tight with the fear of discovery, she bid him a hasty farewell and hurried out into the yard just as Nightrider glided in to land. Galen vaulted from the saddle, and Cara and Breena ran forward to take the reins. "What happened?" demanded Cara breathlessly. "Did you have to fight? Was it wild dragons? Pards?"

Galen tore off his flying goggles, laughed, and shook his head. "You've a lurid imagination, young Cara. No, nothing so dangerous, just firedogs and howlers." He pulled his gauntlets off, chuckling. "They ran like coneys when we arrived." His face clouded. "Mind you, I wouldn't like to face even firedogs and howlers without a dragon at my side. Vicious beasts. What they did to the sheep and kine they managed to catch before we got there . . ." He shook his head. "Still, they didn't have time to kill more than half a dozen beasts before we drove them far into the hills. We gave some of them a scorching to remember us by, too—I don't think they'll be back in a hurry." Looking up, Galen caught sight of Huw standing at the entrance to the stable yard. "Give Nightrider a rubdown, will you?" he said to Cara. "I have to go and report to the Dragonmaster." He strode away through the gathering throng of returning dragons and their riders.

Cara gave Galen's huge mount a despairing look. "Oh, good—another dragon to groom."

Breena sighed. "Ah well, let's get on. If we work fast, we may even be finished before breakfast!"

*　　*　　*

A few hours later Cara was feeling jaded as she did her usual chores. Dragons still needed to be fed and stalls mucked out, even on the day of a showing. Nevertheless, Cara still felt sorry for Drane. She really ought to do more to make him feel welcome, but he didn't seem to be in the stable yard. She hailed Breena. "Have you seen Drane?"

"He's around the back of the stables, taking a barrow of dung to the muck heap."

"Right. I'll just—uh-oh—" Cara caught her breath as a sudden, unpleasant thought struck her. "Breena—you did remember to warn him to be very careful about how he tips—"

She never finished the sentence. There was a loud *THWUMPF*, a flash of light, and a startled cry from behind the stables. Grinning stable hands paused in their work and winked at one another.

Seconds later Drane walked slowly back into the stable yard. His face was blackened, his clothes were singed, and he was covered head to toe in dragon droppings. "It exploded," he said in a dazed voice. "The muck heap exploded. I just tipped out the barrow and it blew up in my face."

Breena stifled a giggle. "Oh, Drane, I am sorry. I should have warned you. You quite often get a buildup of gas in a heap of dragon droppings. If it gets agitated, it can ignite. So you have to be very careful when tipping

out. I forgot that you wouldn't
know that."

Drane wiped glop from his
face. "I didn't think cleaning out
stables could be so dangerous,"
he said mournfully.

"Come on," said Cara,
trying very hard not to laugh.
"I'll show you to the pump.
You can get yourself cleaned
up—but you'd better hurry.
You don't want to be late
for the showing."

By the time Cara had
left Drane shivering under a
stream of ice-cold water and
returned to the stable yard,
the last dragon was being
led down to the show
ground. The yard was empty and the stalls deserted,
except for one—where a young dragon peered up at
the flights wheeling overhead, and pricked his ears forward
at their excited calls. He obviously wanted desperately
to join in. Cara felt a lump come to her throat. Her
poor, beloved Skydancer—the one dragon who wasn't
invited to the party.

She ran across the yard and threw her arms around

his neck. Skydancer keened softly, never taking his eyes from the dragons circling above.

"It's your own fault," Cara told him sternly. The dragon gave her a reproachful look. "Well, it is, you know it is. If you'd just stop being so stubborn and let my da train you, you could be up there with them." Sky's head drooped, and Cara knew that her heart wasn't in the rebuke. "Oh, Sky, I know what it is. You want me to ride you, you don't want anyone else. And I want that, too, more than anything else in the world—but I can't, Sky, I can't."

She stood, hugging Skydancer, until she felt a tug on her sleeve.

"Come on, Cara." Breena's voice sounded in her ear. "They'll be starting soon. Time to go down."

Cara shook her head. "You go. I'm staying here."

"That's no good and you know it." Breena's voice was soft and persuasive. "You'll only mope, and you'll upset your da. And what about Wony? You can't let her down."

"All right." Cara's voice was muffled. "You go on. I'm coming."

Footsteps sounded on the cobbles of the yard as Breena moved away. Cara gave Skydancer a last hug and set off to follow, steeling herself to ignore the dragon's plaintive cries. When she turned at the kitchen door, the lonely dragon was once more peering upward with hopeless longing. It took all Cara's strength not to run back to him.

TACKING UP

Cara went into the bustling house and climbed the stairs to her room with dragging footsteps. Though she wasn't riding, Huw would expect his daughter to dress in honor of the day. The Dragonsdale showing was an annual event, and was taken very seriously. The hard-eyed traders, thrifty farmers, and knowledgeable dragon owners who attended would be carefully scrutinizing everything about the training farm, from the tidiness of its stables to the effectiveness of its training, and comparing it with its rivals before deciding where to buy or place their dragons. In addition, the competitions that would be held were qualifiers for the Island Championships. Dragonsdale's reputation would suffer if its riders did not do well—or if the daughter of the house appeared looking like a scarecrow.

So Cara put on a clean jerkin, respectable breeches, and boots that, though scuffed, were at least not crusted from sole to calf with dragon dung. She dashed cold water over her face and neck, and ran a comb through the worst of her tangles. Cara had never taken too much

notice of her personal
appearance, and today
her heart wasn't in it
at all. After a last,
despairing tug at a
particularly intricate
knot, she gave up
and hurried out of the
house to join the stream
of visitors making
their way to the showing.

Cara left the parade ring by the front gate. To her right, a lane led to the smithy, where Wayland Forgemaster had his wares displayed. Wayland's metalwork—snaffles, buckles, stirrup irons, and all the tools and instruments needed for the riding and care of dragons—was famous throughout the Isles of Bresal, and the forge was surrounded by appreciative buyers. Sparks flew from its chimney, and the air rang to the strike of hammer on anvil.

In the meadow beyond, important visitors were arriving in calashes pulled by dragons. A landing strip marked with gaily colored flags had been set aside for these flying chariots. One by one, they swung gracefully in to land, their skids gouging parallel grooves in the lush grass as their dragons glided a few feet above the ground, and then landed, running, losing speed steadily as the calash came to rest.

The competition area lay on the other side of the Dragonsbeck. Cara crossed the bridge over the stream and followed the road to the show ground to join the housekeepers and stable hands, who were busy with last-minute preparations.

Tents of varying sizes had sprung up all over the short grass like angular mushrooms. Some were white, others gaily striped. One tent had the staff-and-serpent symbol of the Guild of Surgeons emblazoned on its walls. Outside it, serious-looking volunteers rolled bandages and

cut wooden splints, in anticipation of casualties when the competitions began. Lines of bunting flapped in the breeze between the tent poles, and a spiderweb of guy ropes crisscrossed around them, a trap for the unwary.

Food tents were serving bread, cheese, and pies, many varieties of mouthwatering cake, and scones smothered with mounds of cream and jam. Under Gerda's anxious direction, kitchen maids were arranging plates of curd tarts and a huge quaking pudding that wobbled alarmingly on its oversize serving dish as though determined to live up to its name.

Other tents were serving drinks: fruit and nettle teas, dandelion and burdock or ginger beer for the youngsters, heather ale, cider, punch, wine, and mead. Several whole wild boars, brought in by hunting dragons from the Isle of Wildernesse, were roasting on spits over an open fire. Spectators were wandering around the tents or setting up camp in small areas of the meadow for picnics later in the day.

Cara made her way to the paddock, where competitors were milling around. They wore breeches, shining boots, and immaculate full-skirted woolen riding habits, mostly in the green of Dragonsdale. Some were wearing aprons or coveralls to keep their clothes spotless. Most were still carrying their velvet-covered steel riding helmets, which were too hot and heavy to be put on until the need arose.

Cara spotted Drane and went to meet him. At close quarters, she wrinkled her nose. The pump and a change of clothes had done wonders for Drane's appearance but had done little to rid him of a ripe stable-yard odor. He was staring about in confusion and looking miserable.

"Cheer up," Cara said brightly. "Why the long face?"

"Well, let's see," said Drane. "Since I got here I've been nearly fried, head-butted and trampled on by baby dragons, just escaped being torn to pieces by savage scaly bats . . ."

"Wyverns," Cara told him, "not bats."

". . . three-quarters strangled by riding equipment, and covered in exploding dung, and now I'm here and everybody else seems to know what they're doing and I still don't have a clue what's going on!"

Cara remembered her earlier resolution to be nice to Drane. "Well, this is where the show flying is going to be. The novices are going to perform over there in the fun ring." She pointed to a large circle of straw bales. "And see the paddock over there?" Drane nodded. "Well, those hurdles—"

"Those what?"

"The screen things made from woven branches—see?" Drane nodded. "Well, those are sort of temporary stables—that's where the dragons that are competing today wait for their event."

"I thought you didn't make stables out of wood because they'd burn."

Cara gave Drane a surprised look. Evidently he had been listening yesterday. "Temporary, I said—anyway, they're soaked in a special mixture to make them fireproof—"

"What sort of mixture?"

"A sort of ground-up rock and . . ." Cara flushed. "Well—pee, if you want the truth."

Drane grinned at her. "Dragon pee or human pee?"

"Dragon and human." Cara felt it was time to change the subject. "And where the stands are, that's the show arena. It's normally a practice area, but today it's where the main competition will take place."

"Where all those rods and poles and hoops and things are?" Drane stared toward the arena, where competitors were already flying their dragons around hanging poles, under, over, and between precariously balanced rods, and through hoops suspended from ropes and chains high above the ground.

Cara watched the swooping dragons for a moment, her throat tightening with the old familiar feeling of envy and longing. "That's right."

The clanging of a bell rang out across the show ground. "Come on," said Cara. "That's the signal to open the showing. I'd better go and make sure Cloudbreaker's ready for Hortense."

But as Cara and Drane crossed the paddock, they found Wony next to Bumble, struggling under a mountain of tack. The young dragon was standing patiently with an expression on his face that seemed to say, "Here we go again. . . ."

As Wony fought unsuccessfully to hold on to the mass of leather straps, Cara took pity on her. "Would you like help tacking up?" she asked.

Wony gave her a grateful smile. "Yes, please. I get so nervous at these shows—I'm all thumbs."

Cara turned to Drane. "Speaking of which . . . you can help, too; you may as well learn how to put tack on a dragon, rather than tie yourself up in it." Drane colored. "Let's leave the reins and harness for the moment." Cara gestured for Wony to climb onto the wooden mounting block next to Bumble. "Up you go . . . Drane and I will pass you the saddle."

With Drane's help, Cara picked up the heavy wood-framed leather saddle and passed it up to Wony. With difficulty, the small girl heaved it onto her dragon's back.

"Make sure Bumble's comfortable—" Cara broke off, fearing that Wony would resent being given such basic advice.

She needn't have worried. The younger girl smiled and put on a clipped voice. *"A badly fitted saddle will discourage free movement of the wings and lead to a stiffening of the dragon's back. . . ."*

Cara clapped her hands in delight. Wony's mimicry of Mistress Hildebrand was near perfect! The young girl continued, wagging her finger and pouting her lips in the manner of Dragonsdale's Chief Riding Instructor. "*Such discomfiture will undoubtedly have an adverse effect upon the overall performance of both dragon and rider. Do I make myself quite clear, girls?*"

"I'm very glad you remember my advice. I trust you will heed it."

Wony spun around, nearly falling off the mounting block. "Mistress Hildebrand!" she cried. "I . . . er, I mean I . . ." Her voice faded away and her face turned deep red.

"And make sure the breast and belly straps are tightened properly as well. We wouldn't want you slipping off again, would we?" Wony shook her head quickly. "What would people say about my teaching skills if my pupils ended up on their backsides before even taking to the air?" Mistress Hildebrand arched an eyebrow and marched off purposefully toward the judges' tent.

"You could have warned me," protested the crimson-faced Wony as she clambered off the mounting block. "And it's not funny."

Cara stifled her laughter. "No harm done. But she's right; you don't want to end up on your bottom in front of everybody."

"Oh, don't," moaned Wony. "My mother and father are here. I hate them watching me ride; they get so nervous and that makes me nervouser."

"Don't worry," said Cara. She took hold of the strap flapping down the side of Bumble's left flank, bent down, and passed underneath the dragon's belly. Emerging on Bumble's right flank, she flipped up the saddle flap and buckled the strap to the saddle. "Is this tight enough?" she asked Wony. The younger girl bent down, pushed her hand between the strap and Bumble's round belly, and nodded.

"We'll tighten the breast strap once we've got the stirrup irons and leg reins sorted. Drane, pass the head harness, please." Cara pointed at the snakelike coil of dark brown leather fitted with several pieces of shining metal. Drane handed it over and watched intently as Cara threaded the headpiece over Bumble's nose, making sure the ridge band wasn't catching on his eye ridge and the muzzle-band was clear of his nostrils. She then placed the hard metal snaffle in the dragon's mouth. Bumble gave a small hoot and chomped on it distastefully as Cara adjusted the gorge-latch so that it wouldn't chafe his throat.

She took hold of the right leg rein and gestured Wony to do the same with the left. The two girls passed down the dragon's flanks and clipped the reins to the stirrup irons.

"How tight do you like the leg rein?" called Cara.

"Not too tight. Sometimes my legs twitch when I get excited and it sends the wrong message to Bumble."

Drane looked quizzical. "How does your leg send a message?" he asked.

"You control which way the dragon flies by moving your leg," replied Wony.

Cara took over the explanation. "If you pull back your left leg, the dragon turns left; pull back the right, it turns right. The farther you pull your foot back, the sharper the turn."

"And if you want to go down, you pull both your feet backward at the same time," added Wony.

Drane pursed his lips. "So how do you tell the dragon to go up?"

"You use these." Cara held up a long thin piece of leather, which she clipped to the rings set in Bumble's ears. "Ear reins," she explained. "You pull back on these to make the dragon ascend. And you can use them to make the dragon bank left or right, too. Pull left to bank left, pull right to bank right."

Drane was still nonplussed. "What's banking?" he asked.

Cara took a deep breath. "Well, if you want a dragon to turn, there's no point just pulling on the leg reins—all that happens then is that you end up flying sideways." She pointed to the dragons and riders already warming up above the paddock. "When a dragon turns—see, that one's doing it now—it drops one wing tip and raises the other at the same time as it changes direction, so it comes around in a smooth curve. That's banking."

"And the tighter the turn, the steeper you have to bank," added Wony. "Coordination between hands and legs is very important in dragonriding," she added.

Cara smiled. Wony knew her riding theory—putting it into practice was the difficult bit for her. *Still,* she thought, *at least Wony does ride a dragon. I've been watching people ride dragons all my life. I'm sure I could ride Sky if my da would only give me the chance.*

"It all sounds very complicated," said Drane. "Not like riding an ox. I used to do that on our farm. It was simple."

"Oxes don't fly," said Wony.

The next few minutes were spent decking Bumble in a variety of leather straps. Tethers, links, curb chains, and chafe guards were all attached and checked for tautness.

Drane looked on, bemused. "How do you remember where they all go?"

"*Practice makes perfect,*" replied Wony and Cara together. They burst out laughing. "Another of Mistress Hildebrand's sayings," explained Cara. "Do it for long enough and it all becomes second nature." She gestured around her. "See?"

The paddock was a hive of activity. Dozens of show dragons of every breed were being tacked up: Darkeyes like Moonflight with the distinctive dark patches on their muzzles, Finbacks, Bearded Dragons with their luxurious and brightly colored chin scales, Firecrests, and Splaytails. Riders and their helpers were working together in close harmony, attaching, threading, buckling, and tightening. As Drane gazed at the preparations, he noticed how the dragons differed in their reactions to this process: Some stood still, some gave off little hoots, some resisted every addition, snapping peevishly at their riders, and others clawed at the ground, impatient to get into the air. He turned his attention back to Bumble.

"Finished!" exclaimed Cara. "He looks lovely." She turned to Wony. "Now you can put the ribbons on."

Wony smiled, reached into her leather kit bag, and pulled out three lengths of emerald-green ribbon. "Dragonsdale's colors," Cara told Drane. "Every training farm has its own identifying colors. Wony's riding for Dragonsdale, so she's wearing green. Private owners have their own colors."

"Green ribbons look very pretty; they go with my eyes," added Wony as she climbed the mounting block and plaited them into Bumble's crest. "You're the best-looking dragon here today," she whispered into his ear.

"Have you entered your classes yet?" asked Cara.

Wony gave a cry of alarm. "I knew I still had something to do!" She gave a final tug at a ribbon and jumped from the block. "Will you come with me to the judges' tent?"

Cara smiled. "Of course—Drane, you stay here with Bumble." She handed him the reins. "And no taking him for a flight."

"Don't worry—there's no chance of that," Drane muttered as Wony and Cara hurried away. "You wouldn't get me on a dragon for all the wealth in Bresal. . . ."

*   *   *

Cara and Wony joined the queue at the judges' tent just
as Breena emerged from it.

"How's Moonflight?" asked Cara.

Breena smiled. "All tacked up and raring to go. You
know him. He's such a show-off—he loves these events.
How about you, Wony? Ready to take home a rosette
today?" The smaller girl gave a nervous smile.

Cara pointed at the handbill Breena was clutching.
"Can I have a look at the program?" Breena handed it to
her. Cara read:

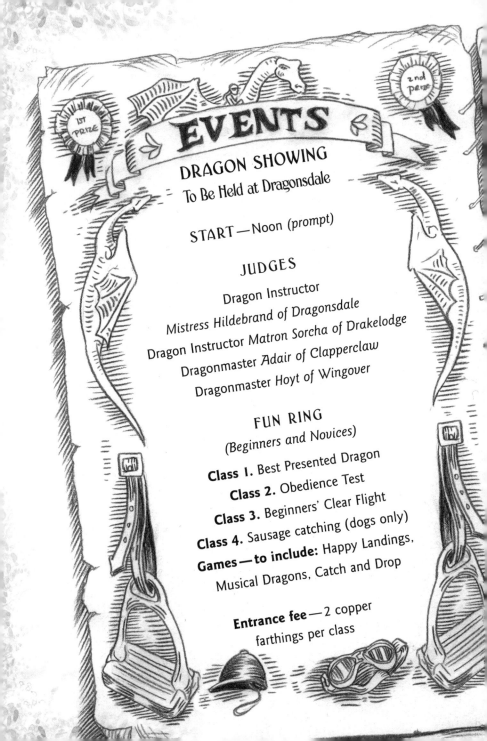

EVENTS

DRAGON SHOWING
To Be Held at Dragonsdale

START — Noon *(prompt)*

JUDGES

Dragon Instructor
Mistress Hildebrand of Dragonsdale
Dragon Instructor Matron Sorcha of Drakelodge
Dragonmaster Adair of Clapperclaw
Dragonmaster Hoyt of Wingover

FUN RING
(Beginners and Novices)

Class 1. Best Presented Dragon
Class 2. Obedience Test
Class 3. Beginners' Clear Flight
Class 4. Sausage catching (dogs only)
Games — to include: Happy Landings,
Musical Dragons, Catch and Drop

Entrance fee — 2 copper
farthings per class

SHOW ARENA
(Intermediate and Senior)

Class 1. Best Presented Dragon
Class 2. Intermediate Clear Flight
Tent Pegging Demonstration Event
Class 3. Senior Clear Flight
Class 4. Senior Time Trial
Class 5. Senior Aerobatics

Entrance fee—2 silver pence per class

Rosettes for clear flights
Trophy and rosettes for each class

Intermediate
and Senior Placings
qualify for
Island Championships

"Which classes have you entered, Breena?" asked Wony.

"Intermediate Clear," said Breena. "And Best Presented. I thought I might as well, considering all the effort I've put into grooming Moonflight!"

"Any idea who else is competing in the intermediates?" asked Cara.

"The usual suspects," said Breena, with a jerk of her head. Cara followed her gaze to see Hortense and her friend Ernestina march out of the tent. Ernestina, a willowy, auburn-headed girl, was smiling slightly: Hortense was furious. "What a fool!" she exclaimed. "I can't believe that stupid judge asked me if I was entering the beginners' class!"

Ernestina's mouth twitched. "Perhaps you should have asked her if she was entering the sausage-catching competition."

Hortense wasn't listening. "I'll speak to Daddy and she'll never be a judge ever again—" Seeing Cara, she broke off her tirade and curled her lip. "Oh, it's you. I hope my dragon is properly turned out. If he isn't, you'll be in trouble." Without waiting for a reply, Hortense turned on her heel and flounced off. Ernestina gave Cara an unreadable glance and followed.

"Well, at least you don't have to worry about Hortense," Cara told Breena. "In all the years she's been competing, she's never flown clear yet."

"No," agreed Breena. "But Ernestina's a good rider. Shame she has Hortense as a friend. . . ."

There was a call from inside the tent. "Next, please!"

Breena gave Wony and Cara a cheerful wave and they entered the tent. Sitting behind a wooden table was Matron Sorcha of Drakelodge. At her right hand sat the recorder—an elderly, slight woman with tied-back white hair. On the table rested a large iron money box, a pot of ink, and several sheets of parchment, above which the recorder held a hovering quill.

"Name?" Matron Sorcha barked out.

Wony froze. Cara gave the smaller girl a nudge.

"Er, Wony."

Matron Sorcha gave a sigh. "Your dragon's name."

"Oh, sorry. Bumble."

The recorder's eyes turned heavenward. Matron Sorcha gave an even deeper sigh. "Its official name, child . . ."

In a small voice, Wony said, "Pollenbloom."

"And the classes you wish to enter?"

"Beginners' Best Presented and Obedience Test, please. Oh, and Musical Dragons."

"Jolly good!" said Matron Sorcha as the recorder scratched at the parchment. "Beginners' Best Presented and Obedience Test it is. The games are free to enter, so that's two classes at two farthings a class—one penny, please."

Wony reached into her pocket, produced a copper coin, and handed it over.

"You'll be called to the ring when it's time—don't be late or you'll lose your place. Next, please!"

DRAGONS ON SHOW

Cara and Wony wandered back to the paddock. The sky was full of dragons being put through their warm-up routines, soaring, diving, and banking in a continual clap and boom of wing beats and hiss of rushing air. There was a buzz of nervous anticipation running through the crowd: As with all dragon events in Bresal, pride, desire, rivalry between stables, and even personal feuds charged the competitive spirit amongst riders and their supporters.

"I wondered where you'd got to," Drane told Cara. "Your father was looking for you—he said you had to make sure that Cloudbreaker was properly prepared."

Cara grimaced. "Hortense has been moaning to him, I'll bet," she said. "I'll have to go, Wony."

The smaller girl's face fell. "I thought you could give me some advice before I go in the ring. . . ."

"Don't worry," Cara reassured her. "I'll be back for your Obedience Test. You'll be fine on your own for Best Presented—just sit on Bumble and answer any questions the judge asks you about grooming. Those ribbons will make all the difference!"

Wony beamed.

"You ought to warm up now," continued Cara. "Put your helmet on and we'll strap you into the saddle."

Wony obediently put on her riding helmet, which looked at least two sizes too large. It flopped forward over her eyes. Cara pushed it back and tightened the chin strap. With some pushing from Drane and Cara, and much huffing and puffing, Wony managed to clamber up from the mounting block, get her right leg over Bumble's back, and plunk herself in the saddle. She placed her feet into the stirrup irons and let Cara adjust the leather straps to the correct length.

When she was satisfied that the leg reins were set right, Cara sprang up onto the block to clip Wony's safety belt and tether into place. "Comfortable but tight enough?" Wony nodded. "Good." Cara passed Wony the hand reins and stepped away. "Correct posture, straight back. Parallel hands and legs slightly bent. That's right. Now off you go—and stay calm!"

Wony gave a little flick of her legs and pulled back with her hands. Bumble began to jog away. Drane and Cara looked on as, with a couple of swishes of his small wings, the rotund dragon took off.

"Right. That's her sorted out."

The bell rang out again across the show ground. Cara

gave a start. "That's the ten-minute warning for Best Presented in the show arena. Come on, we'd better get to the paddock. I need to make sure that Cloudbreaker is pretty enough for Miss High and Mighty. If she doesn't win, I'll never hear the last of it."

"Where have you been?" Cara's father looked up from putting the finishing touches to Cloudbreaker's tack and glowered at his daughter. Drane stepped back to avoid the Dragonmaster's glare. Cloudbreaker craned his neck to nuzzle Cara affectionately, as though apologizing for his earlier peevishness, and gave her a look that said, "I'm going to be ridden by that wretched Hortense shortly, aren't I? What a life."

"Why weren't you around to ready Cloudbreaker?" demanded Huw.

"Cloudbreaker is ready," protested Cara. "I worked on him most of yesterday: descaling, polishing, filing his claws, combing his beard, plaiting his crest. It took me hours."

"Grooming does," said Huw stolidly. "But it's essential. A well-groomed dragon is a happy dragon." But even as he trotted out the old saying, the Dragonmaster seemed to sense that it wasn't helping his argument. He had already inspected Cloudbreaker with an expert eye and knew that what Cara said was true. He hadn't seen a dull scale anywhere on the dragon's hide. "At least you could have been here to tack up," he complained. "I've got better things to be doing with my time—talking business, making sure that customers are happy. Dragonsdale doesn't run on fresh air."

Cara's annoyance spilled over. "Why can't Hortense tack up her own dragon? If she's going to ride Cloudbreaker, she should get him ready. 'Tacking is an essential part of the Trustbond with your dragon.' That's what you always say."

"I also say that fresh air doesn't fill bellies," said Huw acidly, "and my arrangements with Hortense and her father are no concern of yours."

Cara bit back her furious response. She knew that Lord Torin's support was vital to Dragonsdale and that her father didn't like having to bend the rules for Hortense any more than Cara did. And she didn't want any further arguments in front of Drane.

"Oh, goody, he's finally ready." The familiar voice grated in Cara's ear as Hortense appeared at her side, fresh-faced and immaculately dressed in a powder-blue riding habit with lilac facings, her father's colors. There wasn't a speck of dust on her, or a hair out of place—which wasn't altogether surprising, considering that she hadn't lifted a finger to groom or tack up her dragon, Cara thought bitterly.

Hortense inspected Cloudbreaker with the air of someone looking to find fault. It took her just a few seconds before she gave a loud "Oh, no!" and turned on Cara. "You've put the Blacksnape saddle on— I wanted the Springerton. I *told* you I wanted the Springerton."

Cara opened her mouth to tell Hortense that she'd told her no such thing, but before she had drawn breath, her father cut in. "The Blacksnape's oak frame is more robust," he told Hortense. "It gives a rider more support. The Springerton's willow frame is really"—there was a flicker of a pause— "for more advanced riders."

A flash of anger crossed Hortense's face. *Oh, thank you, Da,* thought Cara. But Hortense was not to be bilked of an argument so easily. "Well, what about the rest of the harness? I prefer silver buckles—not brass, not iron—silver. I am the daughter of the High Lord, after all."

Huw's face was like stone. "Silver may look pretty," he said in tones so icy that shivers ran up and down Cara's spine and even Hortense blinked. "But it is not as strong as iron, steel, or brass. Silver buckles may fail. No rider will use them ever again while I am master of Dragonsdale."

The force of his words brooked no argument. Hortense lapsed into a sulky silence.

"I have to go to the arena." Huw handed Cloudbreaker's reins to Cara. "Cara will help you mount." With a nod to Hortense and a glare to Cara, warning her to obey him, Huw strode away.

"I don't need help mounting," said Hortense, when Huw was out of sight. She clambered up the mounting block and, with some effort, settled herself into her saddle. She called down to Cara. "Pass me my whip; it's in my equipment bag."

Cara shook her head. "You won't need a whip for Cloudbreaker. Just warm him up and he'll be fine."

Hortense looked down her nose at Cara, her face twisting into a grimace as if she'd eaten an unripened sourberry.

"Have you ever ridden a dragon?" Cara glared at her and said nothing. "So why are you giving me advice on how to handle a dragon? Pass me my whip!"

Cara reached into the smart leather bag, pulled out a whip, and thrust it toward Hortense. The whip quivered in her hand. Snatching it with a sarcastic "Thank you, Cara!" Hortense gave Cloudbreaker's flank a spiteful crack. She dug her heels into the dragon's side, causing him to shoot upward with an indignant honk. Drane, caught in the backdraft of his wingstroke, was bowled over. Cara watched them go, teeth gritted, too furious to speak.

Drane picked himself up from the ground. "I don't know how you put up with her," he said, rubbing his bruised backside.

Cara's eyes narrowed. "One day, I might not."

Cara had barely recovered her composure before the bell rang to summon the competitors for Best Presented

Dragon (Intermediate and Senior) to the arena. She and Drane took their seats just as the dragons flew in one by one, landing in a cloud of dust and dry grass clippings to the applause of the growing crowd.

"There's Breena," said Cara. She gave her stable companion a wave of encouragement as Breena flew Moonflight into the ring and settled him down in line.

By the time the last competitor had entered the arena, there were more than twenty dragons of various breeds awaiting inspection. A tall, thin figure stepped from the judges' tent into the arena and began a careful scrutiny of the dragons.

Cara nudged Drane. "That's Dragonmaster Adair of Clapperclaw."

Once again, Drane's face had taken on a closed, dark look. "Yes," he said. "I know who he is."

Cara groaned inwardly. Of course Drane knew Adair. His farm had been bound to Clapperclaw, and when it was attacked, Clapperclaw had done nothing.

Dragonmaster Adair picked at the long chin scales of the Bearded dragons, checking for flake; he ran his hands over the red crests of the Firecrest dragons and looked carefully at the large spades of the Splaytails to ensure they had been brushed properly. He also paid particular attention to a Finback dragon, its unusually large dorsal scales standing out proudly.

Adair continued to make his way down the line of dragons. Faced with Drane's silence, Cara found herself giving a rather breathless explanation. "Of course, it's difficult to choose the best presented dragon from so many different types. It's all about how much effort has been put into making sure that they look good and how much attention the rider has paid to a particular dragon's features. For instance, Cloudbreaker's a Firecrest—look between his horns, you can see his red crest. I had to

make sure it was properly cleaned and groomed, as the crest is the first thing a judge will look at."

Drane still said nothing. He stared at the master of Clapperclaw, who had failed to come to his family's aid, and his knuckles whitened.

"Of course," gabbled Cara, "if they all look good and the judge can't decide, then he might ask the riders a

question about grooming or looking after a dragon." *Let's hope he does*, she thought sourly. *Hortense won't know a thing about that.*

In the arena, Dragonmaster Adair finished his inspection. He nodded toward a helper, who passed him three large rosettes of different colors.

"Gold for first, blue for second, and green for third," Cara explained to Drane.

Adair marched up to Breena and Moonflight. Cara jumped up and down in delight. "She's won!" But her delight was short-lived as the judge handed Breena the green rosette.

"Third!" said Cara, disappointed.

The Finback sporting the colors of Wyvernwood was awarded second place. Its rider, a round-faced boy, gave a whoop of triumph before remembering that such displays of emotion were frowned upon. He broke off his celebrations and turned as red as Cloudbreaker's crest.

Dragonmaster Adair turned to the main stand and the eagerly awaiting throng. Cara could have sworn she saw Lord Torin nodding to the judge.

Adair held up the gold rosette. His voice carried across the arena. "The prize for Best Presented Dragon goes to . . . Hortense and Cloudbreaker!" The judge handed the winner's rosette to Hortense. She beamed and acknowledged the smattering of polite applause from the crowd.

"Well, what a surprise!" said Drane bitterly. "Torin

finds in favor of Clapperclaw and Adair—Adair gives Torin's daughter a prize."

"So you don't think all my hard work had anything to do with it?" asked Cara.

"I didn't mean that," protested Drane. "I'm sure you did a good job. It's just—well—it's not fair, that's all I'm saying."

Cara shrugged. "I don't care. At least it'll keep Hortense off my back." As the competitors rose into the air, she took Drane by the arm and led him through the crowd to be in the paddock as Breena and Moonflight circled around and came in to land. "Well done, Breena! Well done, Moony! Third place, better than last time!"

Breena wasn't in a mood for celebrating. "I don't know how she gets away with it!" she fumed. "First place . . . again! And she never grooms her dragon! I know where I'd like to pin her rosette." She handed the green rosette to Cara. "Speaking of which, can you fasten this on Moony's headpiece, please?"

Cara took the rosette, attached it, and gave the dragon's eye ridges a congratulatory rub. "It'll be gold for you in the Clear," she told Moonflight. She grinned at Breena. "And then the Island Championships—for both of you."

"At least Hortense's father can't influence the judges in that!" said Breena. "And just look at that lot of toadies." Cara glanced over to see Hortense being warmly congratulated by her cronies. "I bet she doesn't say thank you, either."

"I don't want to give her the chance," said Cara. "We'll be back to see you fly Clear. Let's go, Drane, we've got to find out how Wony fared."

Cara and Drane arrived back at the Fun Ring to be greeted by a beaming Wony sitting astride Bumble. "I won a rosette!" she cried, pointing at the blue circle of ribbon attached to Bumble's headpiece. "Second prize! The judge said Bumble looked wonderful and he was lucky to have such a caring owner."

"Well done!" said Cara. "I knew you'd do well. Did you have to answer a question?"

Wony nodded. "It was about cleaning tack. The judge asked me what oil I used on the ear reins, and I told her that you should only ever use soap, because using oil makes the reins slippery and you can lose control of your dragon."

"Correct answer." Cara laughed. "You must have been very close to getting first prize."

"The judge said that the only difference between Bumble and Waveflier was the plaiting of the crest. She preferred a double plaiting, and I'd triple-plaited Bumble—I think it looks prettier."

"Ah well, it's all a matter of personal preference," said Cara. "Winning Best Presented means that you've got to get a judge who likes the same things as you."

"Or have a father who is High Lord," said Drane.

A red-faced, stout man standing inside the Fun Ring put a speaking trumpet to his lips. "Competitors for Beginners' Obedience," he boomed out. "Competitors for Beginners' Obedience, please make your way to the ring."

Wony's demeanor changed in the blink of an eye. "Oooh," she moaned. "I feel sick. My mother and father will be watching me. . . ."

"Don't worry," soothed Cara, patting her leg. "You'll be fine."

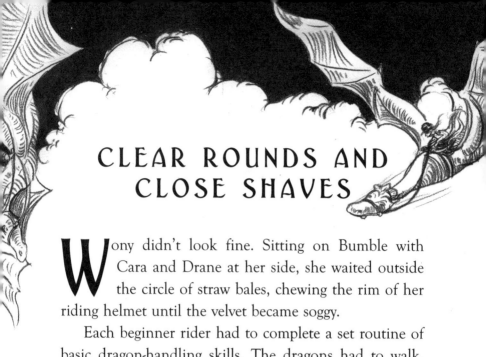

CLEAR ROUNDS AND
CLOSE SHAVES

Wony didn't look fine. Sitting on Bumble with Cara and Drane at her side, she waited outside the circle of straw bales, chewing the rim of her riding helmet until the velvet became soggy.

Each beginner rider had to complete a set routine of basic dragon-handling skills. The dragons had to walk, jog, turn left, turn right, move in a full circle, and come to a halt, before taking off, flying a figure eight around the ring, and landing to complete the display.

As the riders and their dragons came and went, the small crowd of anxious parents and supporters cheered for their

favorites. Cara viewed the proceedings intently, nodding and shaking her head at the various levels of performance and skills.

Drane gave an enormous yawn.

Cara raised an eyebrow. "Tired?" she asked.

"Bored, more like," replied Drane.

Wony's brow furrowed. Cara was incredulous. "How can you be bored at a showing?"

Drane scrunched up his nose and waved his hand. "All this—it's all a bit—" Sensing Cara's hard stare, he broke off.

"All a bit what?"

"Well, what I mean is . . . all the ribbons and the best presented and flying through hoops and everything . . . it's just for girls." Drane winced as he caught Cara's outraged expression.

"Just for girls!" Cara exclaimed. "But everybody wants to fly a dragon!"

"I don't," said Drane firmly.

"Then you must be the only person in Bresal who doesn't! Dragons are important to everyone."

"Are they?" demanded Drane truculently. "If an animal doesn't produce anything you can eat, drink, or wear, what use is it?"

Cara shook her head in wonderment. "What did they teach you at school?"

Drane shrugged. "I hardly ever went to school. My father reckons schools are a waste of time. He says that the only thing you need to know on a farm is how to tell the difference between a he-kine and a she-kine, because if you try to milk the wrong one, you're in big trouble."

Cara's anger abated. "So you don't know anything about the history of Bresal? About the time before humans learned to tame dragons?"

Drane shook his head. "If it isn't to do with farming, as far as my father's concerned, it isn't worth the time of day."

Cara and Wony exchanged glances. Drane really didn't know much. . . .

"Listen," said Cara. "Hundreds of years ago, dragons flew wild in Bresal. Of course, there are still a few wild ones far out to the west—but back then, they were all wild. They terrorized people, scorching crops, killing animals . . . and even humans. People lived in fear of them. Then, according to legend, a young farm girl called Keran came across an injured dragonet next to the body of a dead female dragon. . . ."

"Just like Galen found Sky," said Wony.

Cara nodded and smiled. "Just like Sky . . ." She was silent for a moment, then she continued. "Keran took the dragon home and nursed it, and eventually learned to ride it. That was the beginning of the Trustbond between humans and dragons. Humans began to train dragons, and to see them as allies rather than enemies." Cara gestured toward the ring. "Obedience tests, and all the rest of the competition disciplines at a showing, are based on the skills needed to train a wild dragon. It's all about being one with the dragon; it's all about trust."

"I wouldn't trust a dragon," muttered Drane. "And, whatever you say, there are more girls here than boys."

"Well, yes," admitted Cara. "Boys are more keen on hunting and racing and performing in display teams—"

She was cut off by the announcer's booming voice. "The next competitor is Pollenbloom, ridden by Wony of Dragonsdale."

Wony gave a groan. Cara led her and Bumble into the ring. The small girl urged Bumble forward, saluted

the judges, pulled down her flying goggles, and began her routine.

Cara returned to Drane and gave him a running commentary. "That's a nice right turn; she used her legs well. Sit up, Wony, sit up—that's better. Now the ear reins, not too much, don't confuse him. . . ."

To his credit, Bumble did his very best in obeying Wony's nervous commands as he walked and jogged around the ring.

"Now the takeoff," whispered Cara as Wony brought Bumble to a halt in the middle of the ring. "Come on, Wony, you can do it. . . ."

The young girl pulled back on the ear reins. Bumble gave a couple of flicks of his stumpy wings, causing Wony to lose her balance. Cara gasped as Wony tottered. The surgical crew waiting at the side of the arena rose to their feet in anticipation. Then, with a convulsive heave and a thrust against the stirrup irons, Wony regained her balance and settled herself back into her saddle. Cara gave a sigh of relief as Bumble rose into the air. The crowd burst into sympathetic applause, and the surgeon's assistants settled back into their seats with a disappointed air.

There were no more problems as Bumble flew around

the ring. Finally, Wony landed and guided Bumble to the exit. Cara and Drane met her there.

"Well done, Wony," said Cara, encouragingly. "That wasn't too bad."

"Really?" Wony's anxious face broke into a smile of relief.

"And you didn't fall off," said Drane. He shut up as Cara gave him a cold stare. "Well, she didn't," he said uncomfortably.

"Not too bad for a beginner, young lady." Wony turned to see Mistress Hildebrand nodding appreciatively. "Not good enough for a rosette—a little more work on your balance is needed, but you didn't embarrass yourself . . . or me," she added. "I'll see you in the practice ring next week and we'll work on some long-rein circle flying. . . ." With a nod, the Chief Riding Instructor headed off to the show arena.

"Well, that's praise, coming from her," said Cara.

Wony gave her an anxious look. "Do you think so?"

Cara winked at her. "Better than a rosette any day. And you've still got the games to enjoy."

At that moment a loud cheer went up, and a flight of dragons passed overhead.

Cara looked up. "They're warming up for the Intermediate Clear," she said. "Hop down, Wony, and we'll give Bumble a nice fat moorcock for doing so well. If we're quick about it, with any luck we'll be able to watch Breena win the gold rosette."

*   *   *

By the time Cara, Drane, and Wony had fed and watered Bumble, the Intermediate Clear Flight competition was well under way. They made their way to the stands to join the excited spectators staring upward. High overhead, a dragon was flying at speed toward a large hoop hanging between two lofty masts. At the last moment, it pulled in its wings and shot through the hoop without touching the edge. The crowd burst into enthusiastic applause.

"Nice maneuver," said Cara. "Good tight wings . . ." Her voice faded as she followed the flight with fierce intensity, feeling almost at one with the rider guiding her mount through the aerial forest of obstacles.

The dragon gave two quick wing beats to correct its course, then banked to fly toward two spindly poles. It swept between them, but clipped the left-hand one with its wing tip. The crowd groaned as the pole swayed on its chains.

"Ten penalties," said Cara.

Drane looked puzzled. "What do you mean?"

"In the Intermediate Clear, you have to negotiate the different obstacles," explained Cara. She pointed at each obstacle in turn. "You fly your dragon through the hoops without touching the sides, around the pylons, between those poles, do a knife-edge turn—that's when the dragon's wings are vertical to the ground—then up through the horizontal parallel rods, and dive down to slalom through those hazel wands. That's the most dangerous part of the course because you're so close to the ground. Then it's back up to another hoop and onto those double horizontals to finish. That dragon just hit a pole, so it receives ten penalties."

Wony joined in the explanation. "If the dragon refuses an obstacle, it's five penalties, and if you fly through the obstacles in the wrong order, you're disqualified."

"So what happens if a rider falls off or a dragon crashes?"

"If you just touch the ground, it's ten penalties—but if you crash, then it's the end of the round," said Wony simply.

"The end of the rider and the dragon, too, I should think."

"Drane!" protested Cara.

"I was only asking."

There was another groan from the crowd as the competing dragon clattered into a hazel wand and knocked it spinning out of the ground.

"The winner is the one who gets the fewest penalty points," Wony concluded.

"What if a rider doesn't get any penalties?" asked Drane.

"That's a clear flight," said Wony.

"And what if—?"

Cara could see where Drane was heading. "If more than one rider gets a clear flight, or they get the same number of penalties, they fly off against the clock. Then, if they are still on the same number of penalties, the winner is the one who flies the course fastest."

"That's for beginner and intermediate classes," said Wony. "In the senior classes, there are other competitions."

"Tell me about them some other time," moaned Drane. "My head's spinning as it is."

There was a smattering of applause as the round ended. Cara watched with concern as the dragon came in to make a clumsy landing, having torn a wing sail on the final obstacle. She was relieved to see that Alberich Dragonleech was already on the scene, striding across the floor of the arena to tend to the injured beast with his characteristic long-legged gait, his leather greatcoat flapping behind him. Injuries to dragons and their riders weren't uncommon at a showing, but at least the poor dragon was in good hands.

"Thirty penalties for Mistwing, ridden by Merril of Wyverndale," proclaimed the announcer. "Stormbringer, ridden by Ernestina of Clapperclaw, still leads with the only clear flight."

Cara groaned. "Breena was right—Ernestina's the one to beat."

The announcement continued. "Next to go is Moonflight, ridden by Breena of Dragonsdale."

Cara and Wony cheered and whooped at the top of their voices as Breena and Moonflight flew through the high arch into the ring and circled above the stands, waiting for the obstacles to be reassembled. The rigging crew raced up the masts and hauled on ropes to replace the dislodged rods and poles.

Once the course was ready, Breena touched her hat to the judges sitting in the highest part of the stand and took Moonflight into a warm-up pass before heading toward the first obstacle, a simple arrangement of parallel rods. The dragon went into a shallow dive, and Breena tucked herself into her saddle as they passed between the rods with feet to spare. Then Moonflight was through the first hoop and into a steep banked turn to the pylon pass.

On the ground, Cara was living every moment of her friend's flight—she twisted and turned in her seat as though riding with Breena as she spurred Moonflight through the hoops, around the pylons, and in and out of the hazel slalom wands, banking to left and right, with the dragon's wing tips almost brushing the ground. Moonflight soared upward and through the final hoop. Cara clenched her fists—oh, how she would love to be flying Sky up there! She was snapped out of her dream by Wony's excited shout. "Just the double horizontals to go and she'll be clear!"

Cara, Drane, and Wony watched, hearts in mouths, as dragon and rider flew toward the last obstacle. Nearer and nearer they got, Breena making small adjustments to their approach with gentle pulls of the leg and ear reins.

"Not too fast," whispered Cara.

As if reading Cara's thoughts, Breena slowed Moonflight by a scale's breadth. The dragon glided through the first set of parallels with inches to spare before Breena pulled her up into a steep climb to the final obstacle. Moonflight surged upward with a triple beat of her great wings.

"Easy, easy," mouthed Cara. She needn't have worried. Breena and Moonflight flew between the rods with ease. The crowd burst into a torrent of applause.

"A clear flight for Moonflight and Breena of Dragonsdale!" called out the announcer. "They join Stormbringer and Ernestina of Clapperclaw as the only two clear rounds so far."

"So far," said Cara. "There'll be others."

But she was wrong. Every subsequent rider managed to nudge, knock, or clip an obstacle. With one competitor to go, Breena and Ernestina were the only two riders going into the fly-off.

Wony turned a shining face to Cara. "That means Breena's qualified for the Island Championships, doesn't it?"

Cara grinned. "Yes—but she'll still want to beat Ernestina in the fly-off, if I know her."

The announcer roared, "And now for the final rider of the Intermediate Clear Flight competition . . . the High Lord's daughter, Hortense, riding Cloudbreaker!"

"Oh, honestly!" said Cara. "Everyone knows she's

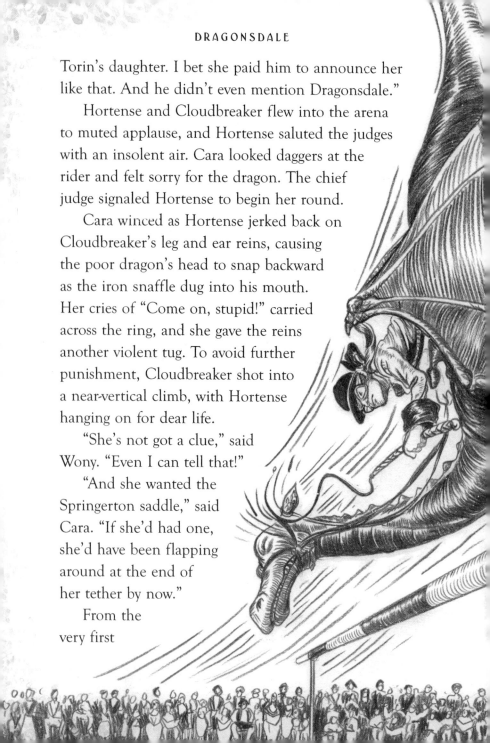

Torin's daughter. I bet she paid him to announce her like that. And he didn't even mention Dragonsdale."

Hortense and Cloudbreaker flew into the arena to muted applause, and Hortense saluted the judges with an insolent air. Cara looked daggers at the rider and felt sorry for the dragon. The chief judge signaled Hortense to begin her round.

Cara winced as Hortense jerked back on Cloudbreaker's leg and ear reins, causing the poor dragon's head to snap backward as the iron snaffle dug into his mouth. Her cries of "Come on, stupid!" carried across the ring, and she gave the reins another violent tug. To avoid further punishment, Cloudbreaker shot into a near-vertical climb, with Hortense hanging on for dear life.

"She's not got a clue," said Wony. "Even I can tell that!"

"And she wanted the Springerton saddle," said Cara. "If she'd had one, she'd have been flapping around at the end of her tether by now."

From the very first

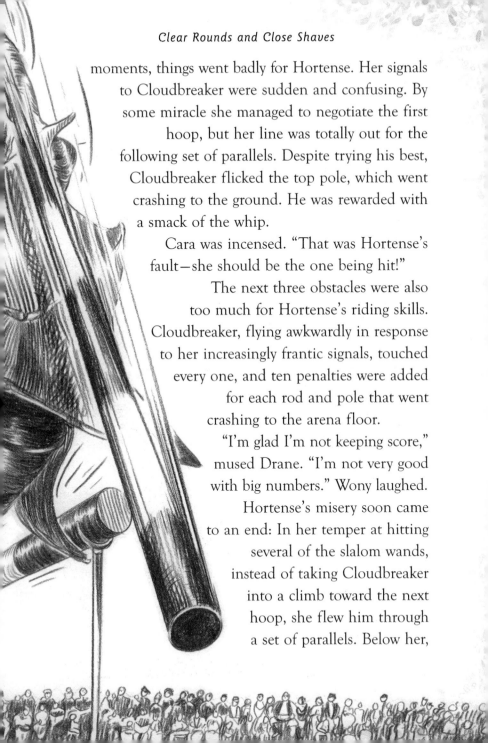

moments, things went badly for Hortense. Her signals to Cloudbreaker were sudden and confusing. By some miracle she managed to negotiate the first hoop, but her line was totally out for the following set of parallels. Despite trying his best, Cloudbreaker flicked the top pole, which went crashing to the ground. He was rewarded with a smack of the whip.

Cara was incensed. "That was Hortense's fault—she should be the one being hit!"

The next three obstacles were also too much for Hortense's riding skills. Cloudbreaker, flying awkwardly in response to her increasingly frantic signals, touched every one, and ten penalties were added for each rod and pole that went crashing to the arena floor.

"I'm glad I'm not keeping score," mused Drane. "I'm not very good with big numbers." Wony laughed.

Hortense's misery soon came to an end: In her temper at hitting several of the slalom wands, instead of taking Cloudbreaker into a climb toward the next hoop, she flew him through a set of parallels. Below her, a bell rang to indicate that she'd taken the wrong course and was disqualified.

As the fuming Hortense turned her disconsolate dragon to glide away from the arena, the crowd remained still and quiet—all except for Wony, who called out loudly: "Serves her right!" Then, realizing that she could be heard, she ducked for cover behind Cara.

The announcer bellowed: "That confirms that third place, and the green rosette, goes to Maeve of Drakelodge with five penalties. The fly-off for the blue and gold rosettes, between Ernestina with Stormbringer and Breena with Moonflight, will commence in ten minutes."

"I'm going to find Breena and wish her luck," said Cara.

Wony nodded. "I'll watch the fly-off with my mother and father. They'll want to see my rosette. And they might have some cake."

Cara laughed. "All right—I'll see you later. Drane, will you keep my seat? I'll be back for the fly-off." Without waiting for a reply, Cara hurried out of the arena and headed across the meadow to the warm-up area.

She found Breena being given some last-minute words of advice by Mistress Hildebrand. "Don't rush," she counseled. "There's no point being a fast-faulter. Better to go steady and fly clear. You've already qualified for the Island Championships, so go out and win this. Win it for Dragonsdale! I'm sorry I won't be able to watch you—I've been put down to judge the best sausage catcher and supervise Musical Dragons, for goodness' sake!" The Chief Riding Instructor turned on her heels and, giving Cara a nod, headed off.

Cara stroked Moonflight's neck. "Good luck."

Breena gave her a grin. "Thanks. Fingers crossed."

The bell calling Breena and Ernestina to the fly-off rang out.

"Here we go!" Breena lowered her flying goggles and urged Moonflight to take off. Cara watched them glide toward the arena, with a familiar feeling of emptiness. It was always someone else, and not her, setting off to fly for Dragonsdale. Cara sighed and began making her way back to the stands to give Breena her support.

"Cara, wait!" Gerda came huffing and puffing from the refreshment tents. "I've only just managed to get away—we've been rushed off our feet! They tell me Breena is in the fly-off against Ernestina. Have I missed it?"

"No, they're just about to start."

Cara fell into step beside the housekeeper. She'd taken only a few paces when a terrible screech made her stop in her tracks. She instantly recognized the sound, and her blood ran cold. Somewhere nearby, a dragon was in distress!

CARA SEES
RED

Cara raced across the cropped grass of the paddock, easily outpacing Gerda. The cries of the dragon were becoming louder and more urgent, and were now joined by other anxious calls as neighboring dragons gave voice to their unease. She reached the dragons' enclosure—and slid to a halt, eyes wide in dismay.

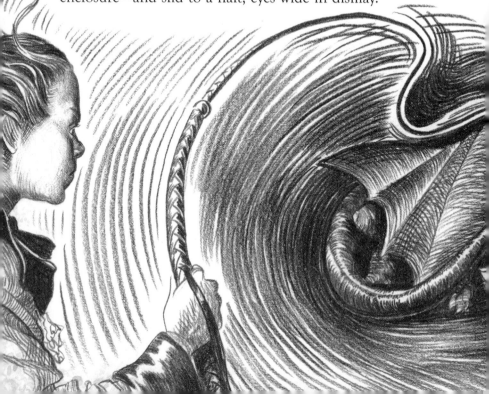

Cloudbreaker was crouched in his temporary stall, cringing like a whipped dog, his wings flattened against the hurdles.

He was hooting with alarm and misery—and with good reason. His reins were tied to a stout peg so that he could not escape, and Hortense was standing in front of him, lashing out furiously with her riding whip. She was beside herself with rage—but not, Cara realized with horror, so much so that she didn't know what she was doing. She was aiming for Cloudbreaker's eyes—always the most vulnerable part of a dragon's armored body—and backing up every vicious blow with an insult.

"You stupid"—*lash*—"lazy"—*lash*—"fat"—*lash*—"slow"—*lash*—"useless"—*lash*—"miserable . . ."

The dragon roared with fright and confusion. Cloudbreaker had never been beaten and had no idea how to react. One blast of his fiery breath would have fried Hortense where she stood, but Cloudbreaker, like all trained dragons, had been taught never to use his flame against a human. It was the most vital part of the Trustbond, never to be broken no matter what the provocation. The mighty creature was powerless.

But Cara wasn't. With a furious cry, she hurled herself at Hortense, snatched the whip from her hand, and threw it away. Then she drew back one balled fist and let fly. . . .

"Ow!" Cara wrung her stinging hand. Hortense went down with a thump. She stared up at Cara in disbelief.

"You hit me!" she said.

Cara gave her a ferocious glare. "Stand up, and I'll do it again."

"You animal!" Hortense lifted a trembling hand to her grazed cheek. A faint smear of red appeared on her white glove. "I'm bleeding."

"Does it hurt?"

"Yes!"

"Good!"

"How dare you?" Hortense's voice trembled. One of her eyes was beginning to close; both were filling with tears. "How dare you?"

"How dare *you*?" demanded Cara. She stood over Hortense, her voice shaking with anger. "You never, never beat a dragon! You coward! You knew he couldn't fight back." She turned back to Cloudbreaker and stroked the agitated dragon's head. "*Shhh, shhh,* it's all right, I won't let her hurt you again."

"He wouldn't fly properly," flared Hortense. "He made me lose the competition. . . ."

"*You* lost the competition! You lost it because you were too lazy to train Cloudbreaker properly, too full of yourself to realize that he knows what he's doing, and too stuck up to listen to anyone who could tell you where you were going wrong. You cruel, spiteful, wicked, ignorant, boar-brained half-wit! You're not fit to ride a dragon."

Hortense scrambled to her feet. She was rapidly regaining her self-control. "But at least I do ride a dragon," she grated. "Not like some people I could mention. I don't moon about after useless dragons that are too stupid to be tamed and too vicious to be ridden. And I'm not too scared to fly a dragon because my mommy killed herself falling off one and my daddy says I mustn't—"

She got no further. With an inarticulate cry, Cara flung herself at her tormentor. Hortense, who wasn't used to having people stand up to her, didn't have a clue about self-defense, and it would have gone very hard with her had Gerda not arrived at that moment to drag the furious Cara away.

A few moments later a crowd began to gather. Hortense was surrounded by friends and hangers-on, all exclaiming with horror at her injuries, making sympathetic noises and casting reproachful looks at her attacker. Gerda was holding Cara's hands against her sides in a grip of iron. She whispered soothing words until slowly Cara began to relax and the light of battle died from her eyes.

"What's going on here?" A lane opened in the crowd to allow the Master of Dragonsdale through to the

center of the excitement.
The portly figure of Lord
Torin trundled after
him, barking pointless
inquiries to late arrivals
who had no more idea
than he of what had
happened.

It was Hortense's
moment. In a tremulous
voice, she said, "It was
Cara—she attacked
me—oh!" And she slid
into her twittering friends'
arms in a well-simulated
faint.

"By thunder!" Lord
Torin wattled like a fighting
rooster, and his pop eyes
blinked alarmingly.
"Violence? Whuff,
whuff! Fisticuffs? Whuff!
Never heard of such a thing. Serious
accusation. Investigate, isn't it? Whuff! Whuff!"

Huw gave Hortense a jaundiced look. He knew all
about her capacity for bending the truth and playacting,
but there was no gainsaying the evidence of her injuries.
He turned to Cara. "Well?"

Cara hated talebearing, but she had no choice. "She was beating Cloudbreaker. . . ."

Hortense's recovery from her swoon was quite amazingly swift. "That's not true! I was gently chastising my dragon, and she came rushing at me like a mad thing and knocked me down. An unprovoked assault. I was in fear of my life. . . ."

Huw's scowl had deepened during this recital, and now he held up one hand in a quelling gesture. Hortense wasn't stupid enough to push her luck with the Dragonmaster. She subsided, snuffling.

"This is not the time or place to establish the rights and wrongs of this business—" began Huw.

"Eh?" Lord Torin's eyes bulged. "Beg to differ, Dragonmaster. Clear case of assault. Whuff! Here's m'daughter, savaged—whuff!—savaged by this she-pard."

"Lord Torin." The Dragonmaster's voice was uncompromising. "The fly-off is about to begin. When it has finished, I shall investigate these events fully, and if I find that the accusation against my daughter is true, I assure you that I shall deal with her. However, at the moment we both have duties to perform. I believe you are to present the prize for the intermediate competition."

"Whuff!" Lord Torin gave Huw a petulant look; his interest in handing out the prize was not nearly as great now that he knew his daughter wouldn't be winning it. But he could hardly say so. "Something in what you say, Dragonmaster." Hortense snorted as indignantly as she dared, but Torin went on. "Mustn't rock the boat. Whuff! Fly the flag, isn't it? Whuff!" He turned to Hortense. "Get some steak on that eye. Prime steak, mind, no scrag end." With a last indignant glare at Cara and a "Whuff!" of protest, the High Lord of Seahaven allowed himself to be led away.

Hortense's friends encircled her like a gaggle of angry geese, hissing and craning their necks, looking around to check that they were attracting the greatest possible degree of attention and sympathy. As they hustled her away, they cast irate glances at Cara, making remarks in voices clearly designed for her to hear:

"Never mind her, Hortense, she's just not worth it!"

"Dragonless wonder!"

"It's just jealousy, Hortense. They gave you a hopeless dragon because they knew you'd win on anything that could actually fly."

"Stupid dragon, they should boil it down for glue."

And above all the other voices came Hortense's penetrating, nasal drawl. "Well, what can you expect from a Dragonsdale hack? They're all as useless as one another."

Gerda quickly threw a restraining arm around Cara. Hortense's voice faded as she was borne away by her gushing admirers. "Anyway, I'm going to make my father buy me a proper dragon of my own; then you'll see some real flying."

Chattering voices replied: "Of course, Hortense." "That's right, Hortense." "You'll show them, Hortense."

At the gate to the paddock, Hortense peered over the heads of her supporters and gave Cara a killing stare. Cara returned it, but made no other response. Then Hortense was gone.

As the crowd dispersed, Cara realized that she was shaking.

"Are you all right?" Gerda said. Cara nodded.

Drane came panting over from the show arena. "Why didn't you come back? I heard there was a fight."

"Hortense was beating her dragon," said Cara. She turned to Gerda. "She was!"

"Of course she was." Gerda gave Cara a quick hug. "Don't let her worry you."

"She'll do something to get her own back," said Cara. "She's plotting already, I know she is!"

"I'll have a word with your father. Don't worry. He knows what Hortense is like. He'll see where the truth is, whatever lies she tells."

"That's not what I mean—" Cara began.

But Gerda was already speaking again. "You'd better make yourself scarce until Lord Torin has gone, and his precious daughter with him. Take Cloudbreaker back to his stable and make sure he's all right. I'll see you later." She bustled off toward the arena.

Drane said, "Would you like me to come with you?"

"No." Drane looked hurt, and Cara realized that she'd spoken more harshly than she'd meant to. "No," she said, more gently, "you enjoy the rest of the showing. There'll be bards and minstrels later, and dancing, I expect. Come on, Cloudy. Let's get you back to your stable." Cara patted Cloudbreaker's muzzle. "Don't worry, Hortense won't be riding you again. Not ever."

She led the subdued dragon out of the paddock and up the hill. Drane watched them go. A burst of prolonged applause came from the show arena, but Cara didn't look back.

"Hi, Cara."

Cara was kneeling in Skydancer's stall, holding the dragon's head in her lap and stroking his eye ridges. She didn't look up. "Hi, Breena." Sky, his eyes closed in blissful satisfaction, crooned a welcome.

Breena leaned over the door. "Is Cloudy all right?"

Cara nodded. "He's pretty miserable—he doesn't really understand what happened—but he's not badly injured. One of his eyes looks a bit inflamed, but it doesn't seem to be hurting him—I'll ask Alberich to look at it tomorrow."

"Good." Breena was silent for a moment. Then she said, "So you missed the fly-off, then."

Cara looked up, shamefaced. "Breena, I'm sorry, I should have asked you straight away. Did you win?"

Breena shook her head. Ruefully, she held up a blue rosette. "I was trying too hard for a fast time. Moony clipped the last parallel. Ernestina flew clear—she won."

"Oh, Breena, I'm so sorry."

Breena shrugged. "I don't mind, really. We put up a good show, and I still qualify for the championships—and Galen will have to find a very good reason not to consider me for the guard flight. Anyway, it's no disgrace losing to Ernestina. She's a good rider. She may be a bit standoffish, but she knows how to handle a dragon, which is more than you can say for Hortense." Breena grinned. "I hear you blacked her eye."

Cara shuddered. "Don't. I shouldn't have hit her like that."

"Of course you shouldn't," said Breena. "You should have hit her a lot harder."

"I'm going to be in the most terrible trouble."

"I don't see why. She was beating poor old Cloudy, lots of people saw her. She asked for it."

"I don't suppose my da will see it like that."

Breena dismissed this with a snort. "Let's just hope she's learned her lesson, that she can't treat our dragons like that and get away with it. Maybe she'll go to Clapperclaw instead." Breena gave the special sniff of disdain she reserved for the mention of any training farm other than Dragonsdale. "I hear they're not particular about who they take—or how they treat their dragons, come to that."

Cara gave her friend a sly look. "We couldn't get that lucky."

Breena chuckled. "That's better. If you've quite finished worrying over nothing, we'd better—"

"Cara!" The strident voice echoed across the stable yard.

Cara pushed Skydancer's head away, causing the dragon to give a mewl of protest, and scrambled to her feet. "Yes, Gerda?"

The housekeeper trundled across the cobbles toward them. "Thought I'd find you here. Come along. Your father wants to see you." Cara groaned. "There's no need to go all tragic on me," Gerda continued brusquely. "I set him right on Hortense's story. He knows what really happened. Wash your face, stand up straight, and tell the truth. You'll be fine. Now get along with you, don't keep the Dragonmaster waiting."

In spite of Gerda's rough words of comfort, Cara made her way back to the house with dragging steps and lowered head, like a condemned criminal on the way to the scaffold. She washed her face as directed, taking as long as she could over a task that she was accustomed to performing in a very few seconds. In spite of this, it seemed no time at all before she found herself standing, with her heart in her mouth and her stomach churning like a neglected stewpot, at the door of her father's study.

Hesitantly, she raised her hand and knocked.

THE
SHRINE

"Come in."

Cara lifted the latch and pushed open the heavy oak door. She stepped into the room and closed the door behind her. Then she turned to face her father, and waited.

The Dragonmaster's study was a small room on the ground floor of Dragonsdale House, with a single window overlooking the parade ring. It was sparsely furnished: a heavy wooden desk with a chair whose cracked leather seat had, over many years, molded itself to the shape of its occupant; two chairs for visitors, standing on a threadbare woolen carpet; and a bookcase whose shelves were overflowing with ledgers and stock books. The walls were covered with various charts, pictures of famous dragons from Dragonsdale, and a calendar from the farm's main feed supplier.

Huw was sitting at his desk, painstakingly writing figures in a ledger. He dipped his quill in the inkpot. Without raising his eyes from his work, he said, "You caused a lot of trouble today, Cara."

Cara couldn't let this pass without comment. "It was Hortense who caused the trouble."

"Hmmm." Huw finished writing, and shook sand over the page to blot the ink before closing the ledger. He looked up. He was wearing the wire-rimmed spectacles he wore only in his office, which always made him look vulnerable. As though aware of this, he took the glasses off and laid them on the desk. "Did you have to knock her down?" he inquired mildly.

"Da, she was beating a dragon. . . ."

"I didn't ask you what she was doing."

Cara subsided. "I suppose not," she said reluctantly.

"You could, in fact, have just taken her whip from her and told her to go away."

"Do you think she'd have gone?"

"We'll never know that, will we? You didn't give her the opportunity." Cara said nothing. Huw sighed. "Cara, I know what sort of person Hortense is. I have good cause to know. I know how . . . difficult she can be. But she is Lord Torin's daughter. You cannot blacken her eye with impunity."

Cara bowed her head. "No, Da."

"Lord Torin is the farm's most important client," Huw went on in the same quiet, measured tones. "He is also High Lord of the Island and owns all the lands hereabout. He has great influence on others. We cannot afford to offend him. And, Cara, take it from me, he is offended."

Cara groaned inwardly. She found it difficult enough to stand up to her father when he was angry, but it was impossible when he was being reasonable. Besides which, he was right. She really hadn't had any absolute reason to knock Hortense down. She tried hard to feel some regret for doing so, but she couldn't. Nevertheless, she said, in a small voice, "Sorry, Da."

Huw grimaced. "I've managed to smooth Lord Torin's ruffled feathers—for now. And I can't blame you for going to the aid of a dragon in distress. But when you see Hortense again, I want you to apologize."

"Apologize?" blurted Cara. "For stopping her from beating a dragon?"

"No, for blacking her eye. I thought we'd established that."

Cara looked as if she were swallowing a spoonful of goose grease, but she said, "Yes, Da."

"Very well." Huw opened his ledger again and retrieved his spectacles.

Cara stared at him. "Is that it?" she said at length.

Huw permitted himself a half smile. "I promised Lord Torin that I'd deal with you. I didn't say how. Consider yourself dealt with. Just don't knock Hortense down again, Cara. For pity's sake, try and stay out of the wretched girl's way."

Cara stifled a gasp, which Huw interpreted correctly. "Yes, she'll be back. One of the things I had to promise Lord Torin was that I'd give her personal tuition to see that she qualifies for the championships."

Cara groaned. This time, her "Sorry, Da!" was heartfelt.

Huw grunted. "At least, with my eye on her, she won't be able to maltreat the unfortunate beast she chooses for her own."

"Da, you can't let her choose from our dragons!" Cara's dismay was unfeigned. "Can't she go somewhere else for one? Clapperclaw would fall over themselves to sell her one! Anyway, she said all our dragons were useless!"

"Unfortunately," said her father drily, "she knows that isn't true, and so does Lord Torin. He's decided his daughter must have her own dragon, and he knows he won't find better than here at Dragonsdale. Hortense will choose from among the eligible dragons in the stables. It's a matter of business."

Cara was too distressed to read the warning sign. She knew from experience that when her father said something was a matter of business, that was an end to the discussion. But she couldn't let matters lie there.

"But, Da, it's not fair!" she blurted. "Hortense is a hopeless rider, and she ill-treats her dragons and never grooms them, and she's to have a dragon of her very own—one of our dragons—and you won't even let me ride Skydancer!"

She knew immediately that she'd gone too far. Her father's face had taken on a stony, closed expression, and his frown darkened. But Cara persisted. "He won't let you train him, or anybody else ride him, because he wants me! We grew up together."

"Cara, that's sentimental nonsense and you know it."

"It isn't," insisted Cara. "We've been friends almost since he was hatched. And we both lost our mothers—"

"That is enough!" Huw shot to his feet. His fist hit the desktop like a thunderclap. "We will not speak of this!"

"Why not?" Cara couldn't stop herself now. "You never want to talk about Mother. Hortense does! She likes to remind me how my mother died, and how scared I am to ride a dragon—"

"So that's it." Huw's voice was softer, though no less grim. "More fool you for listening to ill-natured jibes from the mouth of a spiteful girl. Do you really feel the need to prove yourself to the likes of Hortense?"

"No, but . . ."

"Understand me now!" thundered Huw. "Dragonriding

is dangerous! Your mother was a fine rider, but when her harness failed, all her skill couldn't save her. I lost your mother to a dragon. I will not lose you. You will not ride Skydancer or any other dragon, or take to the air in a calash, now or ever, and let that be an end of the matter. If you mention the wretched beast again, I'll clip his wings and sell him as a watch dragon!"

A knock at the door made the Dragonmaster clench his fists. "What is it now?" he roared.

The door opened a crack and Drane, looking terrified, poked his head through the narrow gap as if afraid of its being instantly taken off. "D-d-dragonmaster," he quavered, "the hatching . . . Starseeker . . . Bran said I was to fetch you . . . he said you wanted to be called . . ."

With a great effort, the Dragonmaster contained his anger. "Very well, Drane. You were right to call me. I'll be there shortly." He reached for his jacket. Drane gave Cara a quick, helpless look and drew his head back like a turtle pulling into its shell.

Huw glared at his daughter and appeared to be about to say something else; but if so, he thought better of it. Contenting himself with a ferocious scowl, he stormed out. The heavy door slammed shut behind him.

Cara stood for some time without moving, trying to control her breathing. She wiped her eyes and took several deep breaths, then crossed the room to the bookcase. Her fingers instantly went to a book, smaller than the rest. She took it from the shelf and opened it.

The book was hollow inside: The center of each page had been carefully cut out to make a space, in which lay a brass key. Cara took the key and returned the book to its place. She left the study, crossed the deserted hall, and climbed the stairs.

On the landing Cara paused outside a door, looking left and right. Finding herself unobserved, she turned the key in the lock, taking great care not to make any noise. She opened the door as quietly as she could and slipped into the room. As the latch clicked into place, Cara locked the door behind her and leaned against it for a few moments, listening. Then she turned.

The room was a bedroom. It was perfectly tidy and free of dust but had the indefinable air of a room that had not been occupied for some time. In fact, Gerda cleaned the room every day, allowing no one else to perform the task. The sheets on the bed were smooth and crisp, and there were flowers in the vase on the windowsill and fresh water in the pitcher on the bedside table.

But nobody lived in this room. Nobody had lived in it for many years. Cara took in every detail of its undisturbed perfection. It was her mother's room, and it looked now exactly as it had looked on the day she died.

Cara crossed the floor as silently as a ghost. She reached out and touched a painted wooden face. The gaily colored toy standing at the foot of

the bed creaked into motion, seesawing back and forth. Cara smiled; it was her old rocking dragon.

Beneath the window, whose soft muslin curtains swayed gently in the air that Cara's stealthy entrance had disturbed, lay a wooden chest. Cara sank to her knees before it as though she were kneeling before a shrine. She opened the lid.

Inside the box lay all the mementoes of her mother's riding career. There were cups and trophies, fading rosettes and sashes, creased and blotched posters and handbills announcing competitions and events, parchment scrolls recording achievements and awards. There were dog-eared notebooks filled with jottings on tack, grooming, and dragon diseases and their cures. There were drawings of dragons, meticulously colored: dragons in flight, watchful dragons, sleeping dragons.

Cara took out each precious relic, handling it reverently, and set it aside. As she did so, her mind traveled into the past. She was four years old, clinging to Gerda's hand as the bearers brought her mother's still body back from the meadow where she had fallen during a practice flight. Her

father had followed them, the
broken harness that had betrayed
her held, forgotten, in his hands,
its silver buckles jingling as he
walked like a man in a nightmare
from which there was no waking. . . .

Silent tears filled Cara's eyes.

At the bottom of the trunk lay a parcel
of waxed cloth. Tenderly, Cara untied the string
that held it together, and folded back the flaps. Inside
the parcel lay a woolen riding habit, full-skirted and
immaculate, in Dragonsdale green. Cara lifted it from its
resting place and held it to her cheek.

It was her mother's show jacket.

Cara rose to her feet. She held up the jacket, inspecting
it for a moment. Then she slipped it on.

For years, the jacket had been a talisman, the object in
her mother's legacy that had made Cara feel closest to her.
It was something to be gazed at, touched with awe, never
to be worn. But not long ago, trembling at her own temerity,
Cara had put it on—and found, to her amazement, that it
was a near-perfect fit. Her mother had been a slightly built
woman, and Cara had grown a good deal in the past couple
of years. She wrapped her arms around herself, holding
the jacket closed, and rocked gently from side to side.

Then her face fell. She took the jacket off and laid it
carefully on the bed. How had she dared to wear it? Her
mother had been a dragonrider, trained, skilled, expert.

She had won many trophies, and not just here on Seahaven—the All Bresal Championship, too. Three times she had been the Champion of Champions, setting the standards against which all others were judged. At every competition, the oldsters, who knew dragons from tongue to tail and wing tip to wing tip, would watch the up-and-coming riders go through their paces, and when asked for their opinion, they would purse their lips and say, "We-llll—she's good. She's very good. But she's no Riona of Dragonsdale."

And Cara had never even flown a dragon. She had been about to join the beginners' class at the moment of her mother's death. Since then, her father had absolutely forbidden Cara from flying. She sometimes felt as though, when her mother had died, her own life—all the parts of it that mattered—had ended, too.

"Oh, Mother," she whispered, running her hands over the jacket. "I love you. I miss you. I wish you were here. Everything would be so different. . . ."

Cara fell across the jacket. She buried her face in it and sobbed, softly, helplessly, for a long time.

So it was that she did not hear the quiet footsteps on the landing as they approached the closed and locked door, paused outside it for a long moment, and then, softly and slowly, faded away.

HORTENSE'S
CHOICE

"**D**ragonmaster!"

Cara looked up, startled, as Mistress Hildebrand's voice echoed around the hatchling shed. The Chief Riding Instructor of Dragonsdale was advancing at a determined march, tapping her riding whip against her boots, her expression radiating fierce disapproval.

Cara and Drane were weighing dragonets again—this time, the hatchlings from Starseeker's clutch. The proud mother was peering fondly at her offspring, making the small hooting noises that Cara always thought of as the draconic equivalent of baby

talk. Maybe Starseeker was saying, "Who's a lubbly, wubbly green, scaly boy, den?"

The dragon would continue to watch over her brood until they were eight months old, at which point she would return to the stables. By this time, in the wild, the dragonets would have learned enough to fend for themselves; in Dragonsdale, however, they would remain in the hatchling sheds, eating their heads off while they grew large and strong enough to carry a human rider.

This was why Cara and Drane (who was handling the tiny dragons with extreme care and keeping a very wary eye on their mother) were weighing the dragonets. Later, they would have to measure them, too—nose to tail, barrel of chest, wing tip to wing tip—and Cara would record the results meticulously in the Dragonsdale records. This morning, her father had summoned her to this task as though nothing had happened between them the previous night. Huw was now leaning over the rail of the stall in which Cara and her reluctant helper were working, watching the dragonets intently as they staggered about on still-shaky legs, squeaking, wriggling their stumpy wings, and occasionally taking an unplanned nosedive into the sand lining the bottom of their pen.

Huw had looked up at Mistress Hildebrand's hail. Cara thought she heard him sigh, but his face was impassive.

The Chief Riding Instructor came to a halt in front

of the Dragonmaster. She planted her feet firmly, braced both fists on her hips, and said in ringing tones, "What's this I hear about Torin's wretched daughter coming here to choose one of our dragons?"

In a voice that sounded a little weary, Huw said, "Your information is correct. Lord Torin will bring Hortense here tomorrow to make her choosing."

"Now see here, Dragonmaster!" Mistress Hildebrand was a tall woman, half a head higher than the stocky Huw. In her anger she seemed even taller, so that she appeared to tower above the Master of Dragonsdale. "I won't have it! The girl's not fit to ride a milking stool!"

Huw didn't flinch. In a quiet voice, he said, "I am well aware of Hortense's abilities as a rider."

"Then how can you even consider allowing one of our mounts to fall into her hands—hands which, I may say, have all the sensitivity of sledgehammers—especially after her treatment of Cloudbreaker? Have you taken leave of your senses?"

Cara saw her father's hands twitch, but his voice remained calm. "Mistress Hildebrand, my business is rearing and selling dragons. I cannot always pick and choose to whom I sell them. It is essential, for the sake of Dragonsdale, that I retain Lord Torin's goodwill."

"You will be sentencing one of our poor beasts to a life of misery and cruelty."

"That's an exaggeration," said Huw heavily, "though I can't say I expect any dragon belonging to Hortense to have an easy life. Nevertheless, if she wants one of our dragons, I am bound to provide her with one."

Mistress Hildebrand drew herself up to her full, impressive height. "In that case, I resign!"

Huw passed one hand across his face in a tired gesture. "Hildebrand, you've already resigned four times this year."

The Chief Riding Instructor looked uncomfortable for a moment, then she rallied. "Yes, but this time, I mean it!"

"Unfortunately, so do I." Huw's voice had tightened; he was obviously coming to the end of his far from inexhaustible stock of patience. "You know perfectly well how impossible it would be for me to refuse Torin—" He broke off, seeming to become aware for the first time that both Cara and the openmouthed Drane were avidly following the course of the argument. Lowering his voice, he took the indignant Mistress Hildebrand by the arm and steered her toward the door of the hatchling shed. "However, we should continue this discussion somewhere more private. Come up to the house. . . ."

He made an impatient gesture toward Drane and Cara, indicating that they should carry on with the task that Mistress Hildebrand's arrival had interrupted, but neither of them moved until the Dragonmaster and the Chief Riding Instructor had left the shed, and their voices had faded into the constant background noise of the stables.

"Phew!" Drane wiped imaginary sweat from his brow and turned to look at Cara. "She seems pretty het up."

Before Cara could reply, Breena raced into the shed and skidded to a halt, panting, by the dragonets' pen. "Cara, have you heard . . . ?"

"Yes."

"I mean, that the Dragonmaster . . . ?"

Cara grimaced. "Yes."

"He can't! He must be mad!" Breena put her hand over her mouth. "Oh, Cara, I'm sorry, I know he's your father and everything, but honestly . . . I mean, he'll be selling one of our beasts to someone he knows is a dragon beater!"

"I don't see what's so special about dragons," said Drane, eyeing the dragonets with disfavor. "Animals get beaten all the time." Drane became painfully aware that Cara and Breena were staring at him as though he'd grown an extra head. He floundered on, "I mean, on the farm, when the oxen are doing the plowing, and they come to a difficult bit where they can't break the ground and they stop—well, if the plowmen think they're not trying very hard, they beat them. . . ." Drane wilted under the girls' glare. "I'm not saying they should, but they do. I've seen it lots of times . . ." He trailed off, intimidated by the waves of icy disapproval radiating from his audience.

Breena opened her mouth to make a furious retort, but Cara put a hand on her arm. "It's not his fault," she said quietly, "he doesn't understand." She turned to

Drane, who was now looking very apprehensive. "Drane," she said kindly, "dragons aren't oxen. An ox is just a brute beast. All it has to know how to do is pull, and the only orders it needs to understand are 'start' and 'stop.'

"But a dragon and its rider have a partnership, founded on trust. A dragonrider has to be able to communicate exactly what she wants her dragon to do, and the dragon has to understand instantly."

Breena nodded, her anger forgotten in her eagerness to make Drane understand. "When you're flying, everything happens so fast. You've got to be able to tell your dragon to dive, climb, bank, turn, roll—sometimes to do three or four things at once—and the dragon has to understand what signals you're giving, and know that they're the right signals." She shrugged. "Though, half the time, what a good rider is really doing isn't so much giving orders as making suggestions."

"But Hortense doesn't understand that," said Cara angrily. "There's never been a Trustbond between her and her dragons. She just tries to bully them into doing whatever she thinks is a good idea at the time, and she's usually wrong. Even when she isn't, she keeps changing her mind and giving the poor beasts confusing signals until they don't know whether they're coming or going. Then when things go wrong, she blames them for everything."

"You mean," said Drane slowly, "she's like my father." Now it was Cara's and Breena's turn to look blank. "My father shouts at everybody all the time," Drane explained, "and he beats the workers when they make mistakes, even though it's usually his own fault for not explaining properly what he wants them to do. And because they're so frightened of him, they make more mistakes than they would if he left them alone. Isn't that the sort of thing you mean?"

"Yes," said Cara, suddenly feeling rather sorry for Drane. "More or less. Dragons are trained to obey human beings, but that doesn't mean a rider can treat a dragon like a slave. If they're to work well together, there has to be a partnership between them—a meeting of minds. That's what the Trustbond is. There must be trust between a dragon and its rider . . . and love." Cara fell silent.

Breena regarded her friend for a moment with concern. Then she shrugged. "Ah well. What can't be cured must be endured, I suppose. But I can't help feeling sorry for whichever poor beast Hortense chooses for her very own."

"She's planning something," said Cara.

"Who? Hortense?" Breena looked startled. Then she gave a bark of mirthless laughter. "You're never going to tell me you're frightened of her."

"Not of Hortense," said Cara quietly. "Of what she might do."

"Like what?"

"I don't know." Cara's voice was low and unhappy. "I've just got a feeling that something dreadful is going to happen."

*   *   *

The night before Hortense's visit had been uneventful. The patrols had not reported any sightings of predators. The firedogs and howlers seemed to have retreated to the lonely moors in the North, far from human habitation. All was quiet at Dragonsdale. But Cara's sense of dread had intensified. She hadn't slept well. She felt slow and stupid, and her morning chores took her longer than usual. She had barely finished mucking out her last stall when the brass bell above the stable block rang out to announce the impending arrival of the High Lord.

Cara abandoned her wheelbarrow in the stable yard and rushed into the house and up to her room. She sloshed water from the pitcher into the bowl beside her bed and gave her face a quick wash before putting on her best blue linen dress, leather belt, and black lace-up boots. She pulled off her hairband and brushed her long red hair in an attempt to make herself half respectable for the choosing.

A quick look in the mirror was enough to persuade Cara that she would pass. She rushed downstairs and out of the front door of Dragonsdale House, onto the parade ring where the Dragonmaster's staff were drawn up in untidy lines, dressed in their best and least comfortable clothes, for the choosing. Breena, standing next to Drane, made a face at Cara as she headed toward her place beside her father.

The five-year-old dragons from which Hortense would make her choice were already lined up as Cara arrived, hot, flushed, and out of breath. Huw gave her an angry look, but before he could tell her off, he was distracted by a commotion at the entrance to the ring. Another dragon was being brought in. The latecomer was fighting against its reins, flapping its wings madly while six stable hands attempted to move it into line.

"Sky!" cried Cara.

"What's going on?" His face flushed with anger, Huw strode across to the struggling hands. "Bran! What are you about? What is that beast doing here?"

The head lad gave Huw a startled look. "But, Master, Miss Hortense sent a message to say that she wanted to see all the five-year-olds—she specifically mentioned Skydancer. . . ."

The Dragonmaster looked ready to burst. "Miss Hortense is not master here! Take him away before—"

The watch-dragon at the gates of the house trumpeted a greeting. Huw groaned. "Too late! Torin's on his way."

"Father." Cara plucked frantically at the Dragonmaster's sleeve. "Let me go to Sky. He won't struggle if I'm with him."

Huw paused for less than a second. Then he nodded. "All right. Be sure you keep him quiet."

Cara raced across the parade ring, hardly aware of the shadow that swooped across it as the calash, pulled by four dragons and bearing the High Lord of Seahaven and his daughter, came in to land in the meadow beyond. "Stop tugging like that," she cried, seizing a rein from one of the struggling stable hands. "All of you! Leave him alone! He's frightened! You're hurting him."

At a gesture from the scowling Dragonmaster, the hands stepped back. Cara immediately began fumbling with straps and buckles. "*Shh*, Sky. *Shh*. It's me. It's Cara. Calm down. Look, I'm taking the harness off. Stop wriggling. It's coming off. See?"

As Cara undid the last buckle, the head harness fell to the ground. Breena stepped forward to snatch it up. She returned to her place and handed the harness to Drane, who held it as though afraid it would bite him. Skydancer immediately quieted and lowered his head to be stroked. Cara scratched at Sky's eye ridges. The dragon settled placidly into his place in line just as Lord Torin's party swept into the parade ring.

Cara was so busy soothing Sky that she missed the formal greeting ceremony with which any visit from Lord Torin was bound to begin. She became aware of her surroundings again only when Hortense began her inspection of the dragons.

The High Lord's daughter was attended by her father and the Dragonmaster. She had also brought along three of her most empty-headed friends, who brayed with laughter at anything Hortense said and simpered outrageously whenever she looked in their direction. She led the party along the line, examining dragon after dragon. Cara noticed that Hortense was holding a brand-new riding whip, and she clenched her fists to stop them shaking.

At length, Hortense reached Cara's end of the line. Her eye was now an interesting shade of purple with a yellow rim. To compensate for this, she was immaculately dressed in a riding habit that was superbly cut and utterly uncreased and spotless. She looked Cara slowly up and down, making it clear that she had noted with disdain every detail of her untidy hair, faded dress, and scuffed boots. Her friends, in the background, whispered to one another and giggled.

"Cara," said Hortense with a smile that made Cara want to strangle her. Knowing her father expected it, Cara made a studied effort to smile back.

"Hello, Hortense."

Huw coughed significantly. As though every word were being dragged out of her like a rotten tooth, Cara went on. "I'm sorry I hit you." She held out her hand.

Lord Torin let out an indignant "Whuff!" but otherwise made no comment. Hortense's friends muttered. Hortense appeared not to notice Cara's hand. In a light, careless voice, she murmured, "Think nothing of it." But the unpleasant smile she gave as she said this did nothing to allay Cara's fears.

Hortense looked past Cara to the dragon at her shoulder. "What do we have here?" she said in tones of ill-simulated surprise. "I didn't expect this one."

Cara looked hard at Hortense. According to Bran, she had asked for Skydancer to be included in the line-up. What game was she playing?

"Skydancer, isn't it?" Hortense continued. "The untamable dragon." She paused for a moment, staring hard at Cara. "Your favorite . . ." Hortense studied Skydancer closely, her expression unreadable. She exchanged a glance with her friends, who nudged one another. Then she looked directly at Cara and gave her a triumphant smirk.

Cara's breath caught. Surely she couldn't . . . ?

Hortense turned away to scan the dragons brought for her choosing. She walked slowly up and down the line, apparently lost in thought, weighing the merits of each, musing over her final choice. Cara sagged with relief.

With the speed of a striking snake, Hortense swung back. Her whip flicked out. She turned to face her father. "I'll have that one."

The end of the whip was pointing straight at Sky.

TEST FLIGHT

For a heartbeat, Cara stood rooted to the spot with shock and dismay. Then she turned to her father in appeal. "No—Da, she can't . . ."

Huw had not moved. His face was like stone. "That will do, Cara."

"But, Da, she doesn't want Sky, not really, she just wants to get back at me—"

"I said, that will do!" The Dragonmaster's voice was icy. "Control yourself, or you will have to leave."

Lord Torin muttered something that began with "Young girls today" and ended with an explosive "Whuff!" Hortense's friends snickered.

Cara made a desperate effort to contain her feelings. Her stomach was churning and she was trembling all over. Let Skydancer go to Hortense? She'd rather die! But what could she do? She cast a horrified look at Breena, who gestured helplessly.

Mistress Hildebrand stepped forward. "Dragonmaster, I protest! You cannot allow this. I shall resign!"

Huw gave her a quelling look. "Unless my memory is at fault, you have already resigned."

"Ah—I was reconsidering . . ." The Chief Riding Instructor's haughty voice faltered. She gave a snort of baffled fury and turned her back on the Dragonmaster. A few moments later, Breena sidled over to Mistress Hildebrand and engaged her in an earnest, whispered conversation.

Huw turned to the High Lord. "Lord Torin, I apologize for the outbursts from my daughter and my staff." Torin gave an affronted "Whuff!" to indicate that he was not appeased. "Nevertheless," the Dragonmaster continued, "I must urge your daughter to make another choice. She may not be aware that this dragon is . . . not fully trained."

Cara held her breath. Surely the High Lord would listen to reason?

"Then why's he out here with the others? Eh? Whuff! Answer me that."

Hanging on to his patience by a thread, Huw said, "A mistake on the part of my stable hands—I had no intention of . . ."

"I'll tell you what it is, Dragonmaster." Lord Torin's foolish face took on an expression of extreme cunning. Lowering his voice to a rumble, he said, "I can see through a stone wall as far as the next man, I hope. Oh, yes. Weren't going to bring this one out, eh? I know what that means! Whuff, whuff!"

Cara glanced from her father to Lord Torin and back again, baffled.

Huw seemed to share her puzzlement. "I'm afraid I fail to understand you."

"Oh, stuff!" Lord Torin nudged the Dragonmaster in the ribs with his elbow and winked at Huw's granite expression. "Come now, we're both men of the world. Whuff!" The High Lord seemed to inflate with self-importance. "Without false modesty, I pride myself on being a pretty good judge of dragonflesh."

Cara gaped at him. Huw's frozen expression said clearly that no modesty, false or otherwise, could truthfully describe Lord Torin as a "good judge of dragonflesh." It was widely whispered that he needed labels to tell one end of a dragon from the other.

"When a Dragonmaster wants to keep hold of a dragon," Torin went on with a smirk, "I know what that means! Oh, yes. Whuff! And a Goldenbrow, too! Very rare, I'm told. Can't pull the wool over my eyes. If you don't want to sell this dragon, he must be something pretty special. Hot stuff, eh? Ha-ha! Hear that? Dragon! Hot stuff! Eh? Eh? Whuff, whuff!" Torin chuckled at his own wit and cunning.

Cara groaned. Lord Torin had managed to get it into his thick head that the Dragonmaster was somehow trying to cheat him by not offering Skydancer. She caught the gloating expression on Hortense's face and the triumphant glances she was exchanging with her hangers-on. Instantly, Cara understood who had planted this idea, and why. She bit back the furious accusation that rose to her lips.

Huw was clearly finding self-control as difficult as Cara was. "Lord Torin, I assure you there is no attempt at deception. The beast is unrideable."

"Then why d'you keep him, eh? Whuff!"

The question stuck in Cara's mind. She found herself wondering why her father, the stern Dragonmaster, had kept trying with a dragon that anyone else would have given up on long ago. Her eyes widened as realization struck. It was because of her, and her love for the wayward dragon, that Huw had allowed Skydancer to remain at Dragonsdale. She felt a sudden rush of gratitude toward her father, which only deepened her despair at the prospect of losing Sky.

"I can ride him, Papa." Hortense was watching Cara, enjoying her distress. "Don't worry about that." The High Lord's daughter radiated an air of arrogant self-assurance.

"There you are, Dragonmaster," said Lord Torin. " 'M sure m'daughter's more than capable."

Hortense's friends set up a shrill chorus of agreement. "Hortense is a super rider." "She can do it!" "She'll show the nasty thing who's boss."

Mistress Hildebrand gave a derisive "Ha!" which Lord Torin chose to ignore, though he gave the Chief Riding Instructor a filthy look.

The Dragonmaster's mouth twitched, but he only said, "Be that as it may, I strongly advise that you choose another dragon."

"I daresay you do." Torin roared with laughter.

Again, Cara looked from the High Lord to her father. She twisted her hands in the fabric of her dress. Her breathing was shallow and painful.

Huw tried again. "My lord, the beast is willful—"

"You're too soft on your dragons." Hortense's nasal drawl cut across the Dragonmaster's voice.

The voices of her toadies rose in unctuous approval. "That's right!" "Absolutely!" "It's a disgrace!"

Huw gave Hortense a look that should have turned her to stone where she stood, but Hortense didn't even flinch. She was in the ascendant, and she knew it.

"Quite right." Lord Torin nodded complacently. "Sorry to be blunt, Dragonmaster, but there it is. Whuff! Common knowledge. Any dragon can be tamed. All it takes is the necessary firmness."

Staring at Hortense with loathing, Cara could guess who had put *that* thought into the High Lord's head, too. She held her breath.

Huw came to a decision. He indicated Skydancer with a jerk of his head. "Saddle him."

Cara gave a stricken cry. "No!"

"Am I to be bated and gainsaid in my own stable?" Huw's voice was savage as he turned on his daughter. "Saddle him, I say."

Cara stood unmoving, paralyzed with fear and dismay. How could she saddle Skydancer for Hortense to ride? Sky wouldn't understand—he'd see it as a betrayal. . . .

"I'll do it." Breena took the head harness from Drane and stepped forward. Her voice was calm and steady.

For a moment, Cara thought that her father would give Breena a tongue-lashing for her interference, but he swallowed his anger. "Very well."

Cara took half a step toward Breena, who shook her head in warning. "Better if I do it," she murmured as she passed. "Sky will only think badly of me, so."

Cara stepped back. She caught Hortense's eye, and the gloating triumph in it made her feel sick and weak.

Breena clicked her tongue comfortingly. "Come on, now." She reached for Sky's muzzle. The dragon drew back nervously. He knew Breena, and liked her—but he didn't like the harness. He blinked, raised his wings, and shook his head.

"Ah, come on, you big soft thing. Nobody's going to hurt you." Breena put her lips close to the dragon's ear and whispered endearments and words of comfort that no one else could hear. Skydancer hardly seemed to notice as she looped the harness over his head and muzzle, and tightened the straps.

"Cara." Cara jumped and looked up quickly. Standing next to her was Mistress Hildebrand. "Don't worry," she said. "Breena knows what she's doing."

"But Hortense is going to ride Sky—and she'll take him away! I'll never see him again." Cara could no longer contain her grief. She clung to Mistress Hildebrand's skirts. "Why is she doing this? Why?"

"Don't be a ninny, Cara," said Mistress Hildebrand sternly. "You know perfectly well why. Hortense wants Skydancer partly because even she can see that he's a superb dragon and partly because she's stupid and arrogant enough to believe that there's no dragon she can't ride. But most importantly, she wants him because he's your favorite, and taking him away is the best way she can think of to hurt you."

With a great effort, Cara kept her rising panic out of her voice. "Mistress Hildebrand—please! You've got to stop this! Can't you speak to my father?"

Mistress Hildebrand sniffed. "I'm sure I don't know why you should think the Dragonmaster might listen to anything I have to say."

"But you're his Chief Riding Instructor. . . ."

"*Was* his Chief Riding Instructor. I am no longer in the Dragonmaster's employ, as I expect you heard him confirm just now." Mistress Hildebrand gave a grim smile and turned her attention back to Skydancer and Breena. "In any case, I wouldn't miss this for the world."

Cara recoiled, shocked and hurt at this betrayal. She realized with dismay that, while she had been pleading with Mistress Hildebrand, Breena, with the help of Bran, had succeeded in saddling Skydancer. The dragon shifted nervously from foot to foot, apprehensive, unhappy, clearly wondering how on earth he'd allowed himself to get into this situation. Still whispering calmly to Sky, Breena led the unhappy dragon to the mounting block. She turned and looked expectantly at Hortense.

With a complacent smirk, which she democratically shared amongst her friends, her proud father, and the folk of Dragonsdale (ensuring that Cara got a double dose), Hortense stepped forward with indestructible confidence. She climbed onto the mounting block, placed her foot in the stirrup iron, and flung herself up to sit jubilantly on Sky's back. Her friends clapped their hands and uttered squeals of encouragement.

Breena leapt onto the block and reached quickly across Hortense as though adjusting her harness. Then she handed over the reins, stepped down from the block, and stood back. She gave Hortense a cheerful little wave.

For a long moment, Sky was too shocked to move. He stood perfectly still, as though unable to believe that anybody could have the audacity to get on his back.

Then he let out an earsplitting roar of fury and took off like a rocket.

Hortense's friends shrieked in dismay. Lord Torin's look of complacence turned instantly to one of almost comical alarm. "What's it doing? What's it doing?" He tugged the Dragonmaster's sleeve. "Master Huw! What's the beast playing at? Eh? Whuff!"

The Dragonmaster, arms folded, watched the bucking, flailing dragon and its screeching rider, and said nothing.

Cara gazed skyward with her heart in her mouth. Hortense was struggling furiously with the reins, and Sky was just as furiously ignoring her. Hortense had no choice but to hang on like grim death, screaming with fury and terror as Skydancer lived up to his name, pirouetting through the air with great thrusts of his wings.

All eyes were turned skyward. Lord Torin was running about like a distraught mother hen, waving his arms wildly and bellowing idiotic orders to which no one paid any attention. Hortense's friends were alternating between having hysterics and screeching pointless advice: "Hold on, Hortense!" "Don't let go, Hortense!" "Watch out, Hortense! You'll fall off if you're not careful!"

Cara realized that Breena had joined her and Mistress Hildebrand. As Sky performed a loop, Breena remarked, "I don't think Hortense is getting on top of the situation." She said this with some relish.

Mistress Hildebrand nodded. "I have a feeling you may be right."

Cara was aghast. "She'll be killed!"

Breena shook her head. "Oh, I doubt it will come to that. I fastened her saddle belt and tether before I let her go." A wistful smile appeared on her face. "After all, we wouldn't want Hortense to fall from a great height and land in a steaming dung heap."

Mistress Hildebrand nodded dreamily. "Oh, no, we wouldn't want that."

"And wouldn't it be awful if all that bouncing and weaving Sky's doing made her ill?"

"What? Like that, you mean?"

Hortense's screams were momentarily stilled as, following a particularly violent maneuver, she was copiously sick.

"Yes, exactly like that." Breena curled her lip in

distaste. "I don't think Sky will be very happy. I daresay he'll feel the need for a bath. . . ."

The same thought had already occurred to Cara. She set off at a dead run, through the gates of the parade ring and pell-mell down the road to Dragonsmere.

She reached the lake just as Skydancer, gliding in from the far end, came in to land, breasting the water aside in hissing waves before diving beneath the surface, to disappear in a rush of foaming water and a cloud of bubbles.

As the water subsided, Cara hopped from foot to foot on the lakeside. "Come on, you stupid girl," she wailed, "undo your harness. . . ."

At that moment, to her vast relief, and that of the other members of the stables who had come pouring down

to the water's edge, Hortense surfaced. She floundered her way to the side as Skydancer rose from the churning waters, beating his wings to raise his upper body from the lake and scream insults at his defeated rider.

Gasping and stumbling, Hortense waded through the mud at the side of the lake. She was draped with weed; her carefully arranged hair hung in rats' tails; her riding habit drooped in sodden folds. Her friends arrived but did nothing useful; they simply milled about at the lakeside, wringing their hands and crying unhelpful things. "Are you all right?" "Your poor dress!" "Oh, Hortense, you are wet!"

Cara reached out to help Hortense to the bank. Furiously, the High Lord's daughter struck her hand away. She appeared to have taken no serious hurt, but she was weeping with rage and fright.

As her father, panting alarmingly, lumbered to the edge of the lake with the Dragonmaster at his side, Hortense drew herself up. Standing calf-deep in the muddy water, her face working with fury, she jabbed a vicious finger at Skydancer, who was still roaring protests from the middle of the mere.

"You saw him! You all saw what he did! He's a rogue dragon! He's wicked — dangerous — evil! He must be destroyed!"

INTO THE HILLS

Cara did not await the outcome of this disaster. She didn't know exactly how much trouble Sky was in, but it was certainly more than any dragon of Dragonsdale had ever been in before. It seemed to Cara quite possible that with Hortense's demands ringing in his ears, and Lord Torin breathing fire, the Dragonmaster would order that Skydancer be destroyed.

She slipped away from the group by the lakeside as unobtrusively as she could, holding her breath lest she should be called back. To her relief, this did not happen. Huw and Mistress Hildebrand were busy trying to pacify Lord Torin, who was calling for towels, hot milk, and a surgeon, punctuating each demand with barks of "Whuff! Whuff!" like an overexcited boarhound. Gerda and Breena were attempting to wring some of the muddy lake water from Hortense, who, now that she had done all she could to condemn Sky, was feigning near-fatal injuries while her friends moaned and wrung their hands. In the confusion, Cara's departure went almost unnoticed.

She ran full tilt around the lake to the reed beds where Sky, having grown tired of screeching defiance at Hortense, was now savagely chomping up huge mouthfuls of marsh plants—a dragon's instinctive reaction to danger, as the half-rotting plants would quickly be digested in his second stomach to produce gas for flaming. Cara approached the munching dragon. "Sky!" she hissed. "Sky!"

Skydancer turned to look at her but did not stop chewing his mouthful of tasty weed. The dragon was in a bad temper. He had submitted himself to the indignity of the harness and the saddle, and then some wretched human had jumped on his back. All his efforts to throw her off had resulted in nothing but screams that made his ears ache, and then the disgusting creature had deposited half-digested food all over him, forcing him to take an unscheduled bath. Even Cara was not in Skydancer's good books this morning. He gave a snort and chomped another mouthful of weed.

"Sky!" Cara raised her voice as much as she dared; she didn't want to attract attention from the melee across the lake. "Sky, come with me." Sky snorted again. "Please, Sky, you've got to. I've got to get you away from here while they're all busy with Hortense. Come on, Sky. Please!"

Something of her urgency communicated itself to the dragon. With very ill grace, Skydancer lumbered from the lake. Cara stepped forward to throw her arms around his head, stepping ankle-deep into the ooze at the water's edge, oblivious to the weedy dribbles from the dragon's chewing mouth, which were staining the front of her dress. She reached out to take the reins, but Skydancer jerked his head away.

"Oh, all right," said Cara, exasperated. "I won't lead you—but follow me, all right?" She beckoned the dragon forward. "Come on, while they're still busy." Cara turned and ran. Skydancer followed, breaking into a lope. Then he spread his wings.

Hearing this, Cara spun around. "No! You mustn't fly—they'll see you. Stay on the ground." She flapped her

hands downward. "The ground! Come on—this way."

Sky grumbled mutinously in the back of his throat. Nevertheless, he furled his wings and trotted after Cara.

Fortunately for the runaways, the land dropped away beyond the reed beds. For a while, they followed the course of the Dragonsbeck as it tumbled over the rocks in a series of small waterfalls. Then Cara turned north and led Skydancer past the Nursery Hollow. Giving the house and stables a wide berth, they headed around the far side of the knoll topped by the pylon marking the northeastern limit of the home flying area. The house and stables grew small behind them as they climbed steadily into the hills beyond Dragonsdale.

The hands in the stable yard were busy taking the other dragons brought out for Hortense's inspection, which had been thoroughly agitated by Skydancer's frantic flight, back to their stables. The party by the lake was

still completely occupied with Lord Torin and Hortense, who was throwing a fainting fit. Thus it was that only Drane, hovering in the background, uncertain of what to do, chanced to notice the distant figures of Cara and Skydancer as they crossed a ridge behind the house and disappeared from view.

When Cara could go no farther, she led Skydancer into a hollow, which gave some shelter from the wind. Sky lay down, breathing quickly from the unaccustomed exertion, his breath making little clouds of steam in the damp, chilly air. Cara sat down with her back against his shoulder and wondered what to do next.

There was no point in going on even if both she and Sky had not been exhausted by their escape. Sky wasn't used to running, and they had come a long way. Cara tried to picture the flying charts she had studied at Dragonsdale. The farm lay to the south of their present position. To the north, the hills continued all the way to the harbor at South Landing, except where they were slashed as though with a giant cleaver by the long inlet of Merfolk Bay. This was a place of ill omen, with treacherous rocks and inaccessible cliffs. In any case, humans and merfolk did not get on; the fisher folk of the Island blamed the merpeople for damaging their nets and stealing their fish. The ensuing struggle between them, undeclared but bitter, had created a gulf between humans and the people of the sea. A fugitive girl and her dragon would find no welcome there.

Nor was any other direction much better. The sea lay to the east; to the west, the River Tumblewater flowed, roaring, through its gorge, beyond which lay only the bleak and dangerous waste of Clonmoor. Cara shivered involuntarily. There was little comfort or shelter to be found that way.

At least, for the moment, she and Sky were safe from discovery. As they had toiled up into the hills, they had been met by a mist descending from the uplands. That mist would by now have reached Dragonsdale, blanketing the house and stables as thoroughly as it was now wrapping itself around Cara and Sky. Even though their disappearance was bound to have been discovered by now, there would be no search for them until it had lifted. Dragons could fly in fog, roaring and listening to the echoes from the land to fix their position, but it was dangerous, and neither dragons nor their riders would take to the air in poor visibility if they could avoid it. In any case, even if a search party did set out, it would be unable to see anything on the ground.

Cara turned to look at Sky. "Well, I hope you've got some ideas about what we do next, because I haven't."

Skydancer crooned affectionately. The journey had given him time to get over his ill temper. He was a little puzzled as to why they were up here on this cold, bleak hillside instead of back in his warm stable, but cold and damp didn't really bother a dragon, and he was with Cara. He stretched his wings and settled himself more comfortably.

"We'd better stay up here for a while," said Cara. "As long as we can, to make sure that Hortense and Lord Torin are out of the way, and to give my da time to cool down." She sighed. "Oh, Sky, what am I going to do with you?"

The dragon nuzzled her cheek by way of response. Then he craned his neck and began to nibble at the belly strap holding the hated saddle on his back.

"Stop it, Sky," said Cara. She pulled at the noseband of the dragon's head harness. Sky grumbled, but left off his gnawing. "I'm sorry," Cara told him, "but your saddle's too heavy and awkward for me to carry, and if I take it off and leave it out here in the wilds, we'll be in even more trouble than we are already. You'll just have to keep it on until we've found shelter somewhere. The trouble is," she admitted forlornly, "I don't know where. This is as far from home as I've ever been." She rubbed a drip from her nose with the sleeve of her dress, which was already turning gray from mist droplets. "I've never even been to South Landing or the Walds. Everyone else at Dragonsdale has—they just beg a lift from a dragonrider or go in a calash, but not me. Oh, why can't Da let me fly?"

Skydancer gave a mournful chirrup.

"And after what you did to Hortense, he's a thousand times less likely to let me fly you than he ever was, even if he doesn't—" Cara broke off. What would her father do with this "rogue dragon"? Would he make good his threat to sell Sky as a watch dragon? Or, to appease Lord Torin, would he actually . . . ? Cara couldn't bring herself to complete the thought.

"Why can't he see it, Sky?" she whispered. "Why can't he see how much he's hurting me—hurting both of us? You'd let me fly you, wouldn't you?" Sky nuzzled her again. "Yes, I know you would. And I'd give anything to fly you. But he's my father. I know how he was when Mother died. You should have seen him, Sky, he was like a ghost, didn't sleep, wouldn't eat. I don't remember much, I was only small, but I know I spent a lot of time in the kitchen with Gerda. And when I was with my da, most of the time he didn't seem to notice I was there, but then suddenly he'd call me to him and take me in his arms and squeeze me until I thought I'd suffocate, and he'd be crying—not making any noise, just big tears rolling down his cheeks. And when I went to ask him if I could start riding, he was so angry. . . .

"And then you came, Sky. You were so small then." Sky gave an indignant hoot. "Well, you were. My da didn't want you from the first. He said Galen shouldn't have interfered, shouldn't have rescued you; he should have left you to the pards, and let nature take its course. He said a wild dragon—even a dragonet a few days old—couldn't be tamed. But I fell in love with you there and then—do you remember?—and I begged him to let us keep you, and

Gerda joined in, and Mistress Hildebrand threatened to resign, and in the end he agreed, and Gerda and I fed you, and I named you Skydancer. We tried to put you with the dragonets from Windflier's clutch, but she kept pushing you out." Skydancer snorted. "She knew you weren't hers. I had to feed you. You spent months in the kitchen sleeping by the hearth, chasing the wyverns and knocking things over until Gerda shooed you out with her broom."

Cara sighed. "But then my da tried to train you, and the fuss you made! You wouldn't wear a harness, wouldn't run or fly on a rein. And when I was with him, you'd look at me, and I knew what you'd have said if you could. I knew you wouldn't have minded if it'd been me training you, if it'd been me who was going to be your rider.

"But it's not going to happen, Sky. My da won't let me, and I can't defy him." Cara's voice lowered. "It would be different if my mother were still here. I miss her so much, Sky, even though I hardly remember her. Isn't that . . . funny . . . ?"

Cara let her head fall onto her knees and wept. After a while she felt something hot and wet splash onto her hand. She looked up, and saw to her astonishment that Sky, too, was weeping—great, hot, draconic tears. Cara threw her arms around Sky's neck and hugged him as hard as her father had ever hugged her. Sky made no protest.

When she had cried herself to exhaustion, Cara nestled down against Skydancer's warm side and fell asleep. His eyes glowing with tenderness, the dragon stretched with great care and enfolded the sleeping girl beneath one huge wing before he, too, laid his muzzle on the ground, closed his eyes, and slept.

LOST IN
THE MIST

Cara awoke with a start.

The mist in the hollow where she and Skydancer had taken shelter was no longer white, but a dark and dirty gray. Cara had no idea how long she'd been asleep, but she felt stiff from lying on the hard ground, and this, coupled with the gathering gloom, indicated that she had lain there for several hours. Evening was coming on, and they were far from home.

"Sky!" Cara struggled to her feet, every muscle protesting. The dragon snorted and half-opened one eye to give Cara a look of reproof. "Wake up, Sky." There was panic in Cara's voice. "We've slept half the day. We have to get back home before dark."

As she said these words, a long, drawn-out howl sounded from the bleak hills surrounding them: the cry of a hunting beast. In the enveloping fog, it was impossible to tell from which direction it came, but it sounded wild and hungry and too close for comfort.

Skydancer shook mist droplets from his wings,

stretched, and lumbered to his feet, grumbling. He didn't
see why Cara was in such a hurry. She'd chosen this spot,
hadn't she? Night was falling, certainly, but darkness held
no fears for a dragon. Skydancer had lived all his life
in the safety of the Dragonsdale stables. He'd been too
young at the time to have a clear memory of the attack
on the nest where he had
hatched, and of his
mother's desperate
fight to save him.

But Cara was
aware, as Sky was
not, that at night,
the hills above
Dragonsdale were
far from safe. As
Galen had told her,
there were unlikely
to be pards this close
to human habitation; though they were an ever-present
threat in the Western Isles, there were few of the
deadly beasts left in the whole of Seahaven, and those
that remained had their ranges to the far north, in the
wild country beyond Lakeland. But there were other
predators—less powerful than pards, perhaps, and
very much less courageous, but just as ruthless, just as
cunning—and in times of hunger, just as vicious. The

farms didn't pay their tithes for nothing, nor did Galen and his riders fly constant patrols in all weathers just for the fun of it. The hills were no place to be caught out after nightfall.

Cara took the dragon's muzzle between her hands. "Sky," she said, very seriously, "we have to get down. Nobody will come looking for us in this mist, and even if they did, they'd never find us. We have to go as quickly as we can, and we mustn't make any noise." She turned to retrace her steps—and realized with a shock that she could no longer remember the direction from which they had come. She looked around wildly. "South," she mumbled to herself, "we have to go south . . ." But which direction was south? In the shadowless mist, no landmarks were visible; every direction looked the same.

Cara fought down her rising panic. One thing was certain: Their path led downhill. If they went down, out of the hills, even if they didn't manage to find Dragonsdale, they would be leaving danger behind them. The creatures that hunted the hills rarely ventured onto the meadows and cultivated fields of the lowlands.

"Come on, Sky." Cara was sure—well, almost sure—that they'd passed that odd-shaped boulder on the way up. With Skydancer trotting behind her, and her feet slipping on wiry, sodden tufts of grass, Cara set off down the hill.

Rocks loomed up in menacing shapes, appearing far larger than they really were in the gray, shrouded world of mist. Sound was muffled: The cheerful trickling of streams was reduced to a sullen gurgle, yet Cara's slithering footsteps and Skydancer's rhythmic padding seemed twice as loud as usual.

Their path twisted and turned, between clumps of gorse and heather and piles of boulders, turning to right and left, sometimes uphill but more often down. Cara tried to stay calm, but their way grew darker as they went, and the mist seemed to press down on them from every side. . . .

The cry she had heard earlier came again. She thought it was more distant this time, but it was impossible to be sure. Night was falling fast by now; they must hurry, hurry. . . . Cara found herself running down a slope so steep she could not stop, springing from boulder to tussock to boulder again, teetering on the edge of a fall with every step, heading into the blank wall of mist at breakneck speed. . . .

Until a great cleft yawned wide before her very feet. Sheer cliffs of glistening black rock fell away beneath her into a terrible cauldron of roiling vapor, and far below, heard but unseen, the vast, crashing roar of the sea.

Cara teetered on the edge, hands clasping frantically at nothing, feet sliding on the slippery grass—her balance was going, she was about to fall into the abyss . . . involuntarily, she let out a shrill, wordless cry of horror. . . .

There was a snap from behind her, the snap of giant jaws clamping firmly shut. She felt a tug at her belt. Even

before she'd realized that Skydancer
had caught the band of tough leather
in his teeth, she felt herself hauled
back from the terrifying brink.

She turned and flung her
arms around Sky's neck. Her

breath came in great, shuddering gulps. Sky gave a concerned warble and nuzzled her shoulder.

"Sky, you saved me!" Cara struggled to control her breathing. Her mind was racing. How could her sense of direction have gone so completely astray? The cleft into which she had so nearly fallen could only be the farthest reach of Merfolk Bay! All the time she thought she had been heading for Dragonsdale, she had in fact been going in totally the wrong direction. They were now farther from home than they had been when they had stopped to rest. And now, darkness was upon them.

"All right," said Cara, more calmly than she felt, "we'll just have to stay here for the night. We'll move back, away from the cliffs, and I can shelter under your wing again, and—"

She was cut off in midsentence by a horrible, juddering howl that seemed to leap out of the dark mist, far away and to their right. Almost immediately, an answering howl came from their left.

"Well, that settles that," said Cara tightly. "We can't stay here to be hunted down." She looked into the dragon's eyes, faintly glimmering in the last of the light. "Sky, will you let me ride you? I don't mean fly—but four legs are better than two on this ground, and your eyes see better in the dark than mine. I'm going to get into the saddle now, all right?" She tapped Sky's shoulder.

The dragon obediently raised his foreleg. Cara hitched her skirt up and stepped onto it. Then she put one foot in the stirrup irons and, somewhat awkwardly, hauled herself upward. Skydancer made no protest beyond a toss of his head. Cara settled herself into the unfamiliar saddle, feeling a rush of excitement despite the peril of their situation. She held the reins loosely. After a moment's hesitation, and without prompting, Sky set off at a steady walk, away from the terrible cliffs and back into the hills.

It was a nightmare journey for Cara. Sitting on Sky's back in the stable, when she was sure her father wasn't around, was altogether different. Keeping her seat on a saddled and moving dragon was much harder and a great deal less comfortable. The rocking motion of the dragon's ambling gait made her feel insecure. At first she tried to use the reins to keep her balance, but soon realized that her inadvertent tugs were confusing Sky, so she tried to hold herself in the saddle with her leg muscles, which were soon aching in protest and chafing against the leather.

She began to feel rather queasy. Clammy tendrils of mist seemed to catch at her hair and clothing. Cara's dress was soaked; her teeth chattered with the cold.

Her ears were pricked for any sound of danger. Several times more she heard the hunting cries of unseen predators: now close, now farther away, now behind, now in front.

Presently, a chill, gray light seemed to suffuse the swirling vapor. Cara realized that the moon must have risen above the mist. The skies, high above their heads, must be clear: The mist was obviously hugging the ground. It was a half-moon, no more, but Cara found that she could see a little. Sky gave a pleased chuckle and began to speed up, more confident of his way in the fitful light. Cara found herself automatically rocking forward as she discovered that failure to match the dragon's motion brought her into rhythmic and painful contact with the unyielding saddle.

Cara was beginning to relax into the rhythm of riding Sky when a sudden, chilling howl erupted from the mist, shockingly close. As it died away, the sound of rushing footsteps could be heard coming directly toward them. Sky reared, spreading his wings in challenge. Cara screamed and thrust herself forward in the saddle, gripping the side flaps with her knees, hanging on to the reins for dear life. The dragon dropped his front feet back to earth. Cara sprawled across his neck, panting, her heart pounding, her legs turned to jelly. Sky crouched, mouth open to roar, muscles coiled to spring as the running shape burst out of the mist.

"Sky! Wait!" cried Cara. "It's a man." Cara flung one leg over Sky's neck and slid from the saddle, down the dragon's shoulder, to catch the staggering runner's arms before he fell.

"Cara?" The voice was familiar, and completely unexpected.

"Drane?"

Drane it was, disheveled, exhausted, half fainting from his exertions.

"What in the Islands are you doing here?" Cara demanded.

"Looking . . . for . . . you." Drane gulped for air.

"Why?" demanded Cara. "You know it's not safe out here. Especially at night!"

"I could ask you the same thing," said Drane with some spirit.

Cara flushed. "Well, yes, but that's different . . . I had to get Sky away from there, and—"

Drane grabbed Cara by the arm. "That's why I came to find you." He took several deep breaths and went on. "Your father is tearing his hair out! At first when he couldn't find you he was furious, but after that, he was out of his mind with worry. He was going to send dragons out to look for you, but then the mist came down, and he found out that all the hunting dogs were away except for Piran Farmer's lurcher, and that's got distemper, so he couldn't track you on foot, either. Cara, you've got to come back."

"I'm trying to!" snapped Cara. "I lost my way in the mist."

"So did I." Drane's face turned pale with remembered horror. Then his grip on Cara's arm tightened so quickly that she gasped. "There's something out there—in the mist—I heard it. It was behind me . . . that's why I was running. It chased me and—"

He broke off as a long, wavering howl burst from the mist directly in front of them. An answering chorus of howls arose from every side, and behind them: those to their left, low and menacing; those to their right, high-pitched and hysterical.

Instinctively, Cara and Drane drew closer together and backed toward Skydancer, who reared, beat the air with his wings, and hissed a warning.

It seemed to have little effect. Eyes appeared from the mist to their left—terrible, burning eyes, coming closer and closer. As they approached, the hunters opened their mouths to bay. A deep red glow, like the inside of a furnace, burned between their savage teeth, and liquid fire dripped from their jaws, hissing as it struck the waterlogged ground.

"Firedogs," breathed Cara.

The mist had begun to clear, tumbling down to the lowlands and leaving the tops of the hills standing out like islands in a white, insubstantial sea. As the vapor retreated, more beasts emerged from their right. These had no fur, but skin like cured leather and a ridge of wicked-looking spikes along their spines. They threw their heads back to give the hysterical howl that Cara had heard earlier.

"And howlers," moaned Drane.

Cara found to her astonishment that she didn't feel particularly afraid.

"They're probably the same packs that attacked Thorngarth," she said. "Galen said his flight had driven them into the hills. Have you got any weapons?"

Drane fumbled with the leather scrip he wore at his belt and drew out a small instrument with a wooden handle and a curved blade. "I've got this . . ."

"A scale scraper?" Cara shook her head grimly. "I don't think that's going to be enough."

A pack of either firedogs or howlers could prove a mortal foe, and Cara and her companions had the misfortune to be caught between rival hunting packs. With Drane beside her and Skydancer at her back, Cara braced herself to meet the attack of the deadly beasts.

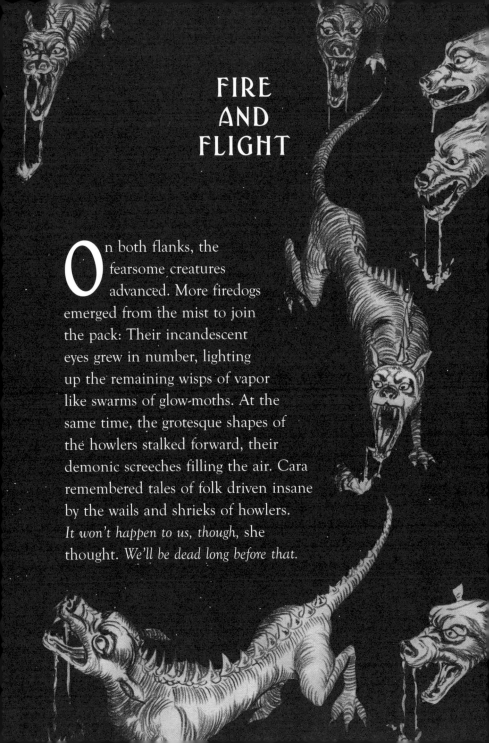

FIRE
AND
FLIGHT

O n both flanks, the fearsome creatures advanced. More firedogs emerged from the mist to join the pack: Their incandescent eyes grew in number, lighting up the remaining wisps of vapor like swarms of glow-moths. At the same time, the grotesque shapes of the howlers stalked forward, their demonic screeches filling the air. Cara remembered tales of folk driven insane by the wails and shrieks of howlers. *It won't happen to us, though,* she thought. *We'll be dead long before that.*

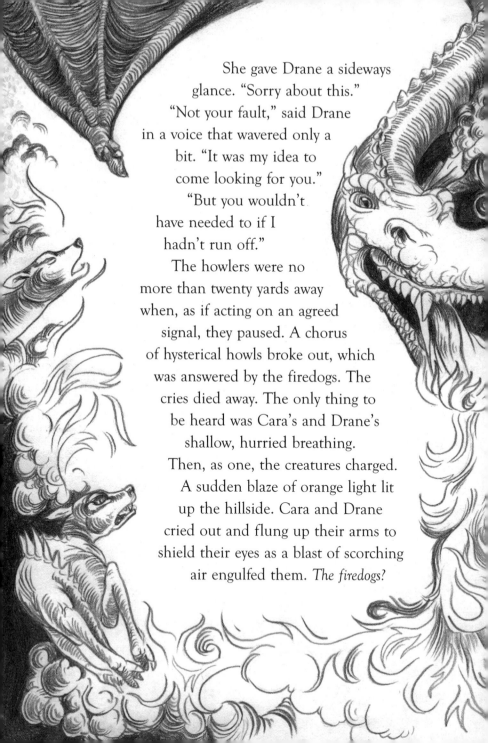

She gave Drane a sideways
glance. "Sorry about this."
"Not your fault," said Drane
in a voice that wavered only a
bit. "It was my idea to
come looking for you."
"But you wouldn't
have needed to if I
hadn't run off."
The howlers were no
more than twenty yards away
when, as if acting on an agreed
signal, they paused. A chorus
of hysterical howls broke out, which
was answered by the firedogs. The
cries died away. The only thing to
be heard was Cara's and Drane's
shallow, hurried breathing.
Then, as one, the creatures charged.
A sudden blaze of orange light lit
up the hillside. Cara and Drane
cried out and flung up their arms to
shield their eyes as a blast of scorching
air engulfed them. *The firedogs?*

thought Cara *distractedly. But they don't actually breathe fire. . . .*

She opened her eyes.

Sky thrust his head forward, mouth agape, and another great swirling tongue of flame shot into the midst of the howlers. Then, with a flick of his head, the dragon turned and sent a third ribbon of flame toward the firedogs. Howling and shrieking, the creatures retreated.

Cara gaped at Sky. "I'd forgotten he could flame!"

Drane stared at her with equal incredulity. "How could you forget a thing like that?"

"Well, I know dragons flame—it's just that I've never seen Sky do it before."

Drane shielded his eyes as Sky shot out another jet of flame. "Get 'em, Sky!" He punched the air in triumph. An acrid smell of scorched grass, burning hide, and smoldering hair hung in the air, as Sky belched out another stream of flame at the loathsome beasts. "Drive 'em off!"

Screeching with pain and fury, the firedogs and howlers turned their backs and scurried away. But once they were out of the range of the dragon's flames, they turned and stood staring and growling. Then they began to creep forward once again.

Sky threw out another spurt of flame. But this time it fell well short of their prowling enemies. The howlers gave a derisive cackle. The firedogs snarled. Drane looked aghast and turned to Cara with a look of desperate inquiry.

Cara shrugged helplessly. "Unfortunately, dragons can't breathe fire for long. They can only store a certain amount of gas in their stomachs. The marsh plants Sky ate earlier have all been digested. He's running out of fuel."

Drane's face fell even further. "That's not good."

The howlers and firedogs were aware of the dragon's limitations. They advanced with more confidence, their primeval hunting instincts telling them that they might after all end up with a good supper.

Sky tried another burst of flame; it was even weaker than the last and petered out into a pathetic dribble.

"That's it," whispered Cara.

Sky curled his head around and pushed Cara toward his right flank. Cara stumbled. "What are you doing, Sky?" Once again the dragon gave her an urgent nudge.

Drane was the first to realize what the dragon wanted. "Those things can't fly, can they?" he said. "You can escape on Sky."

Cara stared at him. "But I'm not supposed to. . . . My da will go mad if I . . ."

". . . get eaten!" supplied Drane. "Go on, before they attack again."

"All right." Cara grabbed the reins. "But we're both going."

"Me? Ride a dragon? Are you crazy? It's dangerous!"

Cara pointed at the howlers and firedogs. "Compared with them?"

"But Sky's only been ridden once," protested Drane, "and remember what he did to Hortense! You go. There's no point in us both getting killed."

"Stop playing the big brave boy."

"I'm not, I'm playing the too-scared-to-ride-a-dragon boy. There's only one saddle—and are you even sure Sky could carry both of us?"

Cara bit her lip—she wasn't. Sky wasn't fully grown, and hadn't flown regularly.

A single firedog, braver than the rest of its brutish companions, broke ranks and ran forward. In a blur of movement, Sky hurled himself at the predator, beating his wings and slashing at it with his sharp claws. With a howl of pain, the firedog retreated to the safety of the pack.

Sky dropped into a crouch and gave Cara a look of mute appeal. She felt herself grabbed around the waist and heaved upward to lie sprawling across the dragon's shoulders like a sack of wheat.

"There's no time to argue! Go!" Drane stepped back as Skydancer beat his wings in a mighty downstroke and, with a roar of defiance, launched himself into the air.

"Sky! Wait! I'm not in the saddle!" Desperately, Cara struggled against the unfamiliar motion; the dragon's slippery hide, constantly rippling beneath her clutching fingers and scrabbling feet from the movement of powerful muscles; the rush of air; her own panic . . . she felt her grasp begin to slip . . . she was going to fall . . .

Drane, now alone, watched the firedogs and howlers advance and waited for the end. "Nice doggies—sit!" he said without much hope.

He was answered by growls and snarls.

Drane remembered the scale-cleaning tool in his hand. He waved it at his attackers. "Good boys—good boys—fetch!" He threw it.

A firedog leapt, and snatched it out of the air with its teeth. It looked deliberately at Drane, and brought its powerful jaws together. The solidly made tool splintered.

Drane gulped.

The predators were beside themselves with rage. They were smarting from the dragon's fire and had now been deprived of two of their victims. Snarling with hate, they leapt forward, jaws wide open and slavering. . . .

Drane closed his eyes and waited for the end.

There was sudden rush of wind, and he felt a violent blow from behind and a pain in his shoulders. He gave an agonized cry. The creatures were upon him!

Then his feet left the ground. Drane opened his eyes, looked around—and realized that he was in the grip of Skydancer's claws, being lifted into the air. The dragon had swooped down to rescue him. The deadly teeth of his attackers snapped inches from his heels before they fell back, howling with disappointed fury.

"Whhaaarrrrrgghhhh!" screamed Drane as the ground sped below him in a blur. "Put me down!"

"What?" called Cara innocently. "Now?"

"Not now! Not now! Later!"

Cara laughed. "Enjoy the ride!"

Far below on the hillside, the firedogs and howlers, denied their human prey, savagely set upon one another in a biting, snarling, bloody melee.

In the air, Cara was ecstatic. Her momentary panic was over—Sky had side-slipped beneath her, arresting her fall and allowing her to get a firm hold, climb into the saddle, and buckle in. And now, she was actually flying! This was so different from riding Skydancer on

the ground. Gone were the jarring footfalls, the clumsy swaying. In the air, the dragon's movements were supple and sinuous. Cara found that she was no longer fighting the motion, but flowing with it, as though she and Skydancer were one creature. Her heart was racing and her eyes were filled with tears—partly from the wind of their passage, but also from her delight that she and Sky were together at last, in complete harmony, doing what they had always been meant to do.

Cara had dreamed of flying for as long as she could remember, but nothing could have prepared her for the glorious reality: the intoxicating sense of freedom, the easy power of the dragon's great wings, the grace of his flight, his effortless mastery of his own element. Cara's ears were full of the clap of wing beats and the hiss and roar of rushing air. Her hair snapped behind her like a banner. The wind sent thin fingers of piercing cold through the impractical dress she had worn for the choosing, and her bare knees felt like lumps of ice, but the discomfort only added to her exhilaration.

She gazed down at the otherworldly glow of the mist-covered ground rushing beneath. She stared up into the dark majesty of the night sky, in which shimmering stars and the half-moon glowed like precious jewels. It was all more wonderful than she could ever have imagined! Skydancer was the prince of this insubstantial world, and Cara was his princess. A smile of sheer contentment spread across her face. She laughed for joy, then leaned forward and patted the dragon's neck.

"Cara," came a plaintive voice from below, "can we go down now?"

Cara gave a start. She had forgotten about Drane. Guiltily, she called, "Take us back home, Sky." As she did so, her jubilation faded and a knot formed in her stomach. Back home—to her father. She was going to have to face the music, and it was going to be very loud.

Cara brought Sky in to land at the foot of the northeast pylon, well away from Dragonsdale House. She didn't want anyone on the farm—least of all her father—to see her riding a dragon.

As they neared the ground, Sky released Drane from his grip. He slumped to the earth as the dragon backpedaled and came to rest.

Cara jumped off Sky and ran to Drane, who was spread-eagled, facedown, clutching at handfuls of the coarse turf. "Beautiful grass," he crooned, "beautiful, safe, firm, steady grass . . ." He rubbed his face in it. Then he looked up at Cara. "That was . . . that was . . ."

"Incredible?" suggested Cara. "Wonderful? Magical? Fantastic?"

"No!" moaned Drane. "Awful. I feel sick."

"Pull yourself together," Cara told him. She held out a hand and hauled Drane to his feet. Keeping hold of his hand, she said, "Thanks for coming after me. It was . . ."

"Stupid," said Drane ruefully.

Cara laughed. "Well—true. But it was also kind, and brave. Thanks." She squeezed his hand and let it go.

Drane looked away. In a better light, Cara would have been able to see the blush she knew was spreading over his thin face.

She became very businesslike. "Listen—we've got to agree on a story that we both stick to. You can't say anything, all right? Not about the howlers, not about the firedogs, and definitely not about me riding Sky. If my da finds out, he'll be sure to sell Sky to Hortense. And you wouldn't want that to happen, would you?"

Drane gave the dragon a sour look and massaged his shoulders. "I'd be heartbroken."

"Drane!"

Hastily, Drane shook his head. "No, no. Of course not."

"So you go back to the house and if someone asks you where you've been, you say you looked for me, but you never found me. Then the mist came down and you gave up your search, but you got lost and you've only just found your way back. All right?"

Drane sighed and nodded. "All right."

Cara took hold of Drane's hand again and recited

an old Bresalian oath. "My hand and your hand, bound together in hardship. Found together in friendship." She released her grip. "Thanks, Drane. Just between you and me. Our secret."

"Our secret," repeated Drane. He shuddered. "Just as long as I never have to fly a dragon ever again!"

Cara gave Drane a head start, then set off to lead Skydancer down the gentle slope of the meadow toward Dragonsdale. They had not gone far before Cara saw the flickering of torches in the thinning mist and heard voices calling her name.

She took a deep breath and stepped forward. "Here! I'm here!"

For a moment, a look of joy and relief spread across Huw's torchlit face. Then it faded, and it was the stern, unflinching voice of the Dragonmaster that called out.

"Cara! Where have you been?" He indicated the stable hands and riders who were now crowding in from all sides. "I've had the whole farm hunting high and low for you for hours!"

As the questions and reproaches flew thick and fast, Mistress Hildebrand took Skydancer's reins from Cara. Breena stepped forward and began to loosen straps. She touched the saddle; her eyes widened and she looked hard at Cara, who groaned inwardly. The seat would still be warm from her riding Sky, and if Breena had spotted that, then so would Mistress Hildebrand—and her father. She shot a look of appeal at Breena, who, without speaking, continued unbuckling the saddle.

"What in the Islands possessed you to go off like that?" her father was asking.

"Skydancer panicked," said Cara quickly. "He'd never been ridden before. No one can expect an untrained dragon to accept a rider without protest, especially one like Hortense."

Huw was not appeased. "Well, where did you get to? I sent search parties out. . . . You were nowhere to be found."

"We were in the hills. I walked Sky to calm him, and then the mist came down, and I found a hollow and waited until it started to clear so we could return," said Cara. She chanced another look at Breena; to her relief, the last buckle was undone. Breena exchanged a meaningful glance with Mistress Hildebrand, took the saddle from Sky's back, and disappeared in the direction of the stables.

"This would never have happened if that lazy, good-for-nothing beast would submit to training." Huw's tone was savage. "I should have packed him off long ago! He's a waste of time, effort, food, and water!"

"You can't send him away," protested Cara, "and you can't kill him just because that's what Hortense wants!"

There was a silence. His relief at having Cara back

finally overcame the Dragonmaster's anger. Like Sky's flame, his temper was used up and burned out. He beckoned to the head lad. "Bran. Take that dragon back to the stables. It's caused me more than enough trouble."

"I'll do it, Dragonmaster," said Mistress Hildebrand calmly.

Huw gave her a hard stare. "I thought you'd resigned."

Mistress Hildebrand drew herself up to her full height and said grandly, "I withdraw my resignation."

"Fine!" said Huw tightly. "Just get the wretched beast out of my sight."

Leading Skydancer, Mistress Hildebrand followed Breena down the hill.

"It wouldn't have happened if you hadn't let Hortense ride him," said Cara fiercely, and immediately she wished she hadn't.

Her father was silent for a moment. Then he turned to the stable hands and gave orders to call off the search. Exchanging wry glances, the hands set off down the gentle slope to the house.

Huw waited until he and Cara were alone before he said, "You will never question my decisions in front of my staff."

Cara hung her head. "I'm sorry, Da."

Huw passed a hand over his face, and when he spoke again, his voice was hollow. "Nevertheless, you're right.

I shouldn't have let Hortense goad me into that rash decision, and put her life in danger. I lost my temper. It was inexcusable."

"It was Lord Torin's fault," said Cara hesitantly. "He insisted."

Huw gave a bark of bitter laughter. "The more at fault Lord Torin is, the more fiercely he'll seek to place the blame elsewhere. What happened today"—he glanced at the lightening sky—"what happened yesterday was not his fault, or Hortense's, but mine, for presenting his daughter with an untrained dragon—which, you will not be surprised to learn, he no longer wants."

Cara stifled a cry of joy.

Huw's torch flickered. "Come. We've all spent far too much of this night away from our beds." He turned to face his daughter. In the guttering torchlight, his face was grim and forbidding. "But understand this, Cara. If that wretched dragon causes any more trouble . . ."

Leaving the sentence unfinished and the threat hanging in the air, the Dragonmaster turned and strode down the dew-frosted slope toward the distant house.

In the great kitchen of Dragonsdale House, Cara had to run the gauntlet of Gerda's reproaches. "Your father was worried sick—we all were. How could you be so thoughtless, disappearing like that?" She banged a bowl of steaming buttermilk pudding in front of Cara so that its contents slopped over the edge and onto the scrubbed wooden surface of the table, letting Cara know that being fed wasn't being forgiven.

"I'm sorry, Gerda," said Cara meekly, "but I couldn't leave Sky up in the hills all by himself, could I?"

"Hmph!" The housekeeper gave her a stony stare for a moment. Then she relented. "Well—eat that up and get to bed. When you wake I'll make you a big breakfast: sausages, mushrooms, eggs . . ."

"Thanks, Gerda." Cara gave the housekeeper a hug, which was returned with interest, took the bowl, and headed for the stairs. But before she made her way to her bedroom, she slipped into her father's study and reached for a small book. . . .

Sometime later, when Cara could hear no more creaking of floorboards, she took a beeswax candle and slipped out of bed. Making her way into her mother's old room, she placed the candlestick on the floor and lit the wick from her tinderbox. Then she unlocked her mother's wooden chest and opened it up.

Carefully placing the books and parchments on the floor, she reached the wax parcel and took out its contents. She hugged her mother's soft green leather riding jacket to her chest.

"Oh, Ma," she whispered. "If only you could have seen me. It was wonderful! Riding Sky—it was like . . . like . . . oh, I can't find the words. But you know, don't you?" Her face set hard with determination. "I know Da doesn't want me to ride, and I know why; he's scared of losing me like he lost you. And I know I should do what he says.

"But if I have a duty to him, I have a duty to you, too. You were a dragonrider. That's what I want to be. Like mother, like daughter. And anyone who sees me ride will remember you. I don't care what it takes, or what I've promised Da, or what the risks are of being found out. I am going to be a dragonrider!"

FLYING FREE

"Cover for me."

"What, again?" Drane groaned. "Cara, do you really think that's a good idea? I'm doing my best to do your chores without anyone noticing, honestly I am. But I'm not used to grooming and mucking out the way you are, and the dragons won't move out of the way for me like they do for you, and I'm sure some of them don't like me, especially Leafscatter. She's been giving me some very funny looks, and I've got blisters all over my hands. . . ."

"You'll be fine," said Cara, who had heard this all before.

"But what if someone asks where you are?"

"Nobody will, except my da, and you just have to tell him what we agreed."

"I don't remember agreeing to anything," said Drane sulkily.

"Don't make difficulties. What will you tell my da?"

"That you think Skydancer has strained his wing," said Drane crossly, "and you've taken him up to Redwater Pool to bathe."

"Very good."

"But what if he doesn't believe me?"

"Why wouldn't he?" demanded Cara. "I've trained Sky to hold his wing a bit awkwardly and look miserable." She chuckled. "I think he enjoys playacting. In fact," she continued thoughtfully, "maybe he's overdoing it. I don't want Da to send for Alberich. He might find out Sky's putting it on, and then I shall have to invent a new excuse."

"Well, what if your da checks whether you're at Redwater Pool?"

"He won't," said Cara. "He'll be too busy." *He's always been too busy,* she added bitterly—but only to herself. "And he won't send any dragons," she continued aloud, "because there are no dragons to send. They're all either on patrol or exercising at this time of day. Nobody will notice I'm gone."

"People have noticed," said Drane heatedly. "Breena knows something's up—and Gerda—and Mistress Hildebrand—and Wo—"

"But they won't say anything," said Cara firmly, "and neither will you."

Drane tried to stare Cara down, failed, and sighed heavily. "Oh, all right!"

He watched discontentedly as she slipped a head harness onto Skydancer—who was holding his wing out in a pitiful way and uttering pathetic little hoots of discomfort at every step—and led him quietly out of the stable yard.

When they
were well out of sight of the
house, Cara tapped Sky sharply
on the muzzle. "You can stop
shamming now," she told him. "There's nobody to see.
Honestly, you're such an old fraud."

Skydancer looked pleased, obviously considering
this to be a compliment. But he folded his wing
properly and ambled eagerly behind Cara as she led
the way to an abandoned shepherd's hut in the hills.
She dragged open the sagging door and brought out
a worn saddle and harness that she had appropriated

from the tack room several days ago. Expertly, she began to fit them. Skydancer—crooning happily in anticipation—crouched as low as he could to allow Cara to lift the saddle onto his back without the aid of a mounting block, then rose so that she could fasten the belly strap.

Cara quickly fitted the reins, despite being hindered by the nudges Sky kept giving her to hurry up. "Keep still, silly," she admonished the excited dragon. She clipped the final strap into place. "There. Done!"

She stepped up onto Skydancer's eagerly proffered foreleg, swung herself up into the saddle in an easy movement, and fastened her safety harness.

Half a second later, Sky's wings unfurled and swept into a powerful downbeat, and Cara and her beloved dragon took to the air.

"Have you seen Cara?"

Drane jumped and dropped his shovel. Hurriedly he snatched it up and turned to face the glowering Dragonmaster, guilt etched into every line of his face. "Nnnooo . . . ," he quavered.

Fortunately Huw was not looking at him but at the dragons wheeling overhead, racing one another between and around the four great pylons surrounding Dragonsdale. "She shouldn't have left you to do her work for her."

"I don't mind, Dragonmaster."

Huw fixed Drane with a look. "Do you not? But I do, apprentice Drane. You are supposed to be working under supervision until you have thoroughly understood your duties."

"Yes, Dragonmaster," said Drane meekly. Feeling that this was not enough, he offered, "I think she said something about Skydancer having strained a wing, and she was going up to Redwater Pool to bathe it in the hot springs . . ." He trailed off uncomfortably. The Dragonmaster was giving him an extremely distrustful look.

"Do not try to deceive me," growled Huw. Drane felt his belly churn and his legs turn to water. "I know perfectly well what my daughter is doing." Drane gave an involuntary whimper, which was fortunately drowned by the protesting roars of a dragon that had been balked in its passage around the northwest pylon. "She's off somewhere with that wretched dragon of hers," continued Huw, "moping like a lovelorn milkmaid because I won't let her fly." Drane almost fainted with relief. "As if I haven't enough to concern myself with, pacifying Lord Torin and his daughter because of that dragon. When she comes back," said the Dragonmaster, "you will tell her I want to see her immediately." He strode off.

Drane's legs gave way and he collapsed into a sitting position. Then he groaned aloud as he realized that his seat was the wheelbarrow into which he had just shoveled the droppings from Leafscatter's stall.

Cara laughed with pure delight as Skydancer swept through the air with slow beats of his powerful wings.

When she and Skydancer had begun their secret flights, Cara had been content to sit passively in the saddle, reveling in the thrill of flying at long, long last, hardly daring to touch the reins, letting the dragon fly them wherever he would. But Skydancer, though he might resent it from anyone but Cara, was used to human guidance, and sadly at a loss when it wasn't forthcoming. His early flights with Cara had been short, with Sky merely gliding a little way and then landing and turning to her with an inquiring look as much as to say, "Well? Where to now?"

So Cara had started to give the dragon gentle hints with the reins, steering him to left and right, increasing and decreasing speed, gingerly learning to coordinate hand and leg movements to show Sky how sharply she wanted him to turn and how steeply to bank.

They always flew low, beneath the horizon from Dragonsdale: in the hills where Cara, Sky, and Drane had met the firedogs and howlers, and across the roaring Tumblewater and the boggy wastes of Clonmoor. They took great care to avoid all human habitation—though, had they flown over some isolated farmstead or croft, their chances of discovery would not have been very great. Dragons were such a familiar sight in the skies above Seahaven that practically no one looked up when one flew overhead, and the few who did would be unlikely to realize that Cara and Skydancer were wicked renegades, absolutely forbidden to do what they were doing.

Cara's first flight by night had been wonderful, but it had been like floating in another, unreal place, far removed from the everyday landscape of the Islands. By day, the exhilaration of flight was no less, but to it was added the warmth of the sun, the patchwork of clouds, the thrill of seeing the landscape flash by beneath them so fast that its details were blurred, and the moments of sheer awe when she and Sky would crest a ridge and a sudden, unexpected vista would open out before them, as though they were being gifted with a whole new world, full of endless possibilities. . . .

With Cara's gentle hands on the reins, Skydancer swooped between barren crags and skimmed hillsides where the glorious pinks and purples of the heather's

summer flowering were giving way to the sere browns of
autumn. They flew along the course of winding streams
that splashed over rocks a few feet below, between valley
sides that almost brushed Sky's wing tips. Reaching the
gorge of the Tumblewater, Skydancer side-slipped down
into the great chasm and zigzagged between the towering
walls of naked rock, his wings misting from the spray of
the roaring torrent beneath. A rising rain dashed against
Cara's face, tingling, its coldness making her gasp.

 The shock of the water cleared Cara's head,
reminding her that this flight had a purpose beyond
mere enjoyment. She and Sky were easy
together, and the Trustbond that had always
existed between them was deepening
with every flight. They were
learning a great deal about
each other—but they
weren't yet a team. Cara
still sometimes gave
signals that Sky
misread—or

even, through
lack of experience,
asked the dragon to
do things that were
unwise, dangerous, or
downright impossible: to bank so hard that
he might flip into a spin, or to climb so steeply that
he would stall. They both still had much to learn.

Pulling back easily with her hands, Cara
signaled that she wished to climb out of the gorge.
She steered Skydancer closer to the cliffs on their
right, to take advantage of the updraft that would
lift them effortlessly over the rim. Once they were
clear of the chasm, she scanned the sky for clouds
beneath which she would also find a rising
current. Spotting a likely candidate, she urged
Sky toward it, and on reaching it, began
to wheel in the column of warm air, the
dragon's wings hardly beating as he spiraled
upward and the landscape dropped away.

Cara's breath came faster. It was

time to start work on the riskier maneuvers. Now that they had some height, she would try a roll.

She waited until they were flying straight and level. Then, without giving Sky a signal to turn, she pulled back on the right ear rein, urging him to bank. Sky obeyed, as he had done many times before, but this time, Cara did not release the pressure. Sky tilted his wings at a steeper and steeper angle, until they were almost vertical. His shoulder muscles stiffened in hesitation, and then, intuitively understanding what his rider wanted him to do, the dragon resumed banking until his wings were vertical to the ground. Still the roll continued, until a few seconds later, Cara, her feet tensed into the stirrup irons, the safety belt straining against her belly, was flying upside down.

Sky completed the roll, his wings moving back to vertical, to a steep bank, and on until he and Cara were once more in level flight.

Cara gave a whoop of excitement and thumped Sky exultantly on the side of his neck. "That was great—let's do it again!"

For the rest of the morning they practiced rolls: fast rolls, slow rolls, hesitation rolls—in which Skydancer would pause for a second or two at varying points in his revolution—developing their skills, blissfully happy in their joy of flying and of each other.

As the sun approached its zenith, Cara turned back toward the distant shepherd's hut. On the way there, they landed at Redwater Pool, and Skydancer splashed happily about in the warm, sulfur-smelling water. At least now Cara would be telling the truth if she had to claim that this was where they'd been. She was still too in love with flying to feel much guilt about deceiving her father.

That would come later.

CHARM
OFFENSIVE

For several days, Cara's early morning rides with Sky continued undiscovered. She had explained her absences to her father by continuing to plead the excuse of Skydancer's "strained wing"—which Sky demonstrated by flapping about and groaning so piteously that Huw's suspicions, if not allayed, were at least slightly eased. So, while her father's attention was turned to the business of flying out strings of racing dragons, putting the formation riders through their paces, and preparing the show riders for the Island Championships, Cara and Sky continued to slip away to the shepherd's hut, where Cara would saddle and harness Sky before taking to the air.

They had discovered a hidden valley, bleak and barren, with a lake at its bottom whose black waters looked sinister and uninviting. But unlovely as the valley was, it had the advantage of being concealed from prying eyes by hills on every side. Here, they would spend an hour or two flying up and down, trying out new maneuvers, honing their skills, cementing their understanding. Then, before she was missed, Cara would return to Dragonsdale just as Drane was finishing her chores of mucking out the stables and feeding and watering the dragons.

In her newfound happiness, Cara had completely forgotten Hortense. But Hortense had not forgotten Cara, and had

certainly not forgiven her. And as for the wretched dragon that had made her look foolish in front of her father, her friends, and the whole of Dragonsdale . . . Hortense burned for revenge.

She was not enjoying her training with Huw, who was a stern taskmaster and very apt to find fault. He had mercilessly dissected her riding style with critical remarks about her seat, her posture, her handling of her mount, and her lack of sympathy with it. She was forbidden to ride Cloudbreaker (who hissed a warning whenever she appeared in the stable yard) and was now partnered with an old and very experienced female Finback. Valeweaver was really past her show-flying peak, but though she was normally of placid temperament, she would stand no nonsense. She had an iron mouth when she chose, and would turn her head with shocking suddenness to snap at Hortense's hands or feet if her rider took liberties. And she knew the obstacles in the show arena inside out—certainly better than Hortense did—and could thread through them without guidance.

So Hortense found herself following the dragon rather than leading it, a situation she was not used to—and which her pride found hard to stomach. And the Dragonmaster was always with her, correcting a hand position here, a foot signal there, making her fly the same obstacles again and again. He would accept no excuses, no "nearly rights." Each exercise or evolution went on until rider and dragon had repeated it perfectly at least five times, and then they would go on to the next.

"I don't know why you're bothering," Hortense said sulkily during one such session. "This horrible dragon takes no notice of me, anyway. She'd fly the course even if I just sat on her back and did nothing."

"This course, yes," said the Dragonmaster coldly. "But it is a practice course. Competition courses always differ, so if you want to qualify for the Island Championships, you will have to guide your dragon. And I promised your father that is what I would teach you to do. Again!" And the exercise continued.

Hortense would not have put up with this sort of treatment from anyone else, but her father had been seriously displeased by her performance at the showing, and his confidence in his daughter's flying abilities had been dealt a blow by her failure to control Skydancer. So she had no choice but to defer to the Dragonmaster, but that didn't mean she had to like it. The sessions were long, and Hortense was always saddle-sore by the time she had finished. Not only that, but Huw insisted she groom her own dragon, and stood over her to make sure that she did so. Naturally, Hortense blamed both of these misfortunes on Cara.

But her increased time in the Dragonsdale yard did have one unexpected benefit for Hortense. She soon realized that Cara was not very often about, and she determined to find out why.

*   *   *

"Come and sit down. You must be exhausted."

Drane looked around, trying to see who Hortense could possibly be talking to. Since there was no one else within sight or earshot, he was forced to the astonishing conclusion that it must be him.

Hortense was early for her lesson with Huw. She was immaculately dressed, as she usually was before flying—though these days, her sessions with Valeweaver and the Dragonmaster often ended with her looking hot, tired, and thoroughly disheveled. She was perched primly on the low wall surrounding the well in the center of the stable yard, smiling at Drane in a disturbingly winsome manner.

Drane was thoroughly mystified. Hortense had never so much as looked at him before, let alone smiled at him. In fact, in Drane's experience, smiling at him was an activity that few girls seemed anxious to pursue. He was also aware that, as he was coming to the end of his—or rather Cara's—morning chores, his clothes were liberally spattered with mud and dung, and he smelled very strongly of sweat and the stable.

Hortense tapped the wall beside her with her riding whip. "Come here, I said," she snapped, in a partial return to her usual manner.

Drane hurried over and perched on the very edge of the wall, while Hortense, getting a whiff of Drane's powerful personal aroma, wrinkled her nose involuntarily. However, she quickly composed her features into a smile, and said in a much more friendly voice, "Poor Drane. I think it's so unfair the way Cara forces you to do her work for her."

Drane, reminding himself that Hortense had had no objection at all to Cara's grooming Cloudbreaker for her, gave her a guarded look. "Do you?"

"Of course—I mean, here you are slaving away, while she's gallivanting off doing—whatever it is she does."

"Oh, I don't mind," said Drane uncomfortably.

"But it isn't right—especially as she's always lecturing—er—people about not doing any work, and now she's not doing any herself."

Drane said nothing, but looking down at his dirty, blistered hands, he couldn't help but feel that Hortense might have a point.

"I mean, look at your poor hands." Hortense took one of Drane's poor hands and held it between her immaculate white gloves, in much the same way as she might pick up something a wyvern had brought in. (After all, she reminded herself, she could always burn the gloves.) She stroked the hand with a look of deep sympathy.

Drane gawped at her. What was Hortense up to?

"You don't like me, do you? I can tell." Hortense gave Drane the "under the eyelashes" look that always worked on her father. "I'm not really a bad person, you know."

"Aren't you?" said Drane incredulously. Then, realizing that this might not be exactly tactful, he hurriedly said, "I mean, no. Of course not."

"People around here just don't understand me." Hortense permitted herself a refined sniffle. "It's not easy, you know, being the High Lord's daughter."

Since Hortense had always got everything she wanted, immediately and without question, Drane couldn't help thinking that actually it must be extremely easy being the High Lord's daughter, but he didn't say so.

"People are jealous of me, you see."

"Are they?"

"Yes. I get pretty lonely sometimes."

As Drane felt pretty lonely himself, pretty much all of the time, he began to feel some sympathy for Hortense, and to wonder whether he might have misjudged her.

"People here aren't very kind," said Hortense in woebegone tones. "I expect you've found that, too."

"Cara's been kind to me," said Drane loyally.

Hortense raised her eyebrows. "If you say so, though I wouldn't call it kind to leave you here to do all her work while she goes off on her own."

"Oh, she doesn't go on her own," said Drane without thinking. "She takes Skydancer with her." Immediately after the words were out, he wished them back.

But Hortense gave no sign of noticing how near Drane had come to breaking a confidence. "I wonder where she goes?" she said casually.

Drane was on safer ground here. He saw nothing wrong with letting Hortense in on Cara's prepared story. "She goes up to Redwater Pool, to bathe Skydancer's wing. He's strained it, you see."

"Really?" Hortense let go of Drane's hand, looked up—and suddenly rose to her feet. "That can't be right—look, that's Skydancer up there, flying with Cara!"

Drane, too, looked up, appalled. "What? No! It can't be! She's not supposed to fly anywhere near . . ." He stuttered to a halt, suddenly aware that for once, there wasn't a single dragon in the sky, and that Hortense was eyeing him with a triumphant smirk. "I mean, she's not supposed to fly at all . . . what with Sky's bad wing . . . and everything . . . ," he concluded lamely.

Hortense turned on her heel and strode off. Making up to that oaf Drane had produced better results than she'd dared hope for. The imaginary dragon had been a shot in the dark, but it had worked. Her suspicions were confirmed: Cara was flying Skydancer. But where? Drane had said something about Redwater Pool—maybe that was a good place to start. . . .

"I'm sure she suspects something."

Drane had told Cara about Hortense's interrogation immediately after supper. He hadn't expected her to be pleased, which was just as well, because she was furious.

She glared at Drane. "Do you mean you told Hortense where I was?"

"Well, yes—no! I mean, not where you really were."

"I don't see why you had to tell her anything at all!"

"She was being nice to me. I was confused! I told her the story you cooked up for your father."

"That's all right, then."

"No, it isn't." There was a pleading note in Drane's voice as he tried to warn Cara to be careful without revealing how he'd almost given the game away. "She's got it in for you, Cara, you know she has. Couldn't you just be careful and stop—?" Cara made urgent shushing motions and Drane lowered his voice. "Stop . . . you know . . . at least for a bit. . . ."

"I'll think about it," said Cara. She was on edge. She'd decided to do something risky, and the last thing she wanted to deal with was a display of nerves from Drane. "Now, please, give it a rest! And don't say anything to anybody—no matter how nice they pretend to be." She strode away, leaving Drane feeling foolish and rather hurt.

Breena came to stand beside him. "What was that about?"

Drane said, "Hortense is sticking her nose in where it's not wanted. I think she knows—or very nearly—what Cara's up to."

Breena didn't pretend to misunderstand him. "I hope you warned Cara to be careful."

Drane shrugged angrily. "You can try, if you like. She won't listen to me."

He slouched away. Breena didn't move. Her eyes, fixed on the door through which Cara had just slipped out into the night, were full of concern.

Some hours later, Cara sat astride her fully harnessed dragon at the entrance to the practice ring, her heart beating fast. She had bribed the watch dragon into silence with a brace of hares from Gerda's store, and had waited until the watchman had gone to answer a call of nature, before sneaking Sky out of the stable yard. The moon was nearly full, which made the obstacles in the ring quite visible now that Cara's eyes had become accustomed to the darkness, though she hoped that she and Sky would be far enough from Dragonsdale House not to be seen.

Cara and Sky had developed a good understanding over the past few weeks. They were working well as a team, conveying their intentions to each other almost as much by intuition as by any physical signal. But up to this point, Cara had never flown Sky through obstacles. Now, with Dragonsdale asleep, she would risk it. Taking a deep breath, she pulled gently back on the ear reins, and Sky took to the air.

She flew the slightly bemused dragon around the course, showing him the obstacles—the parallel rods, the vertical poles, the hoops, the pylons—talking to him constantly in a quiet, confident voice. She did this three times, telling Sky what a clever dragon he was, how he mustn't mind these silly old rods and things—a wonderful flier like him could find his way between them with no trouble at all.

At length she banked Skydancer around and lined him up for the first obstacle—the horizontal parallel rods. "Come on, Sky," she said, "let's go." She leaned forward, pulling back on the foot reins and squeezing with her knees, encouraging the dragon into a shallow dive to increase speed. Sky held his wings out in a glide, and Cara felt her mouth go dry as the obstacle seemed to leap from the ring and rush out at them.

Skydancer sped toward the rods with apparent confidence—but at the last moment, his nerve failed him, and he backed his wings to lose speed before climbing steeply to fly over the topmost bar.

Cara reined him in and went into a wide turn. "Don't worry, silly," she said in reassuring tones. "Those rods look solid, but they're as light as anything. You won't hurt yourself if you touch one." She set Skydancer at the obstacle for a second time. Gritting her teeth, she urged him forward.

At the last moment, Cara crouched in the saddle, and this time Skydancer drove on, straight between the rods. Cara thought they were clear, but a claw of one of the dragon's trailing hind feet touched the bottom rod, which clattered to the ground.

Cara patted Skydancer's neck. "Good boy, you nearly had it—remember to keep your legs tucked up and your tail straight, and we'll get through next time." She brought Skydancer to a hover, landed in the center of the ring, unbuckled her belt and tether, and slipped off the dragon's back. She ran across to replace the pole—and stopped in dismay. She would have to climb the masts that supported the rods to replace the fallen one, but how could she possibly replace both ends at the same time? She hadn't thought of that!

"Hello." The quiet voice from the darkness sent an icy chill through Cara's whole body. "Need a hand?"

THE RECKONING

There was a horrible silence. Cara's heart pounded against her ribs. Then a slim figure stepped out of the shadows.

"Breena!" Cara fought to control her ragged breathing. "You gave me a fright!"

Breena grinned. "And how did you think you were going to replace that big heavy rod all by yourself, so?" She picked up one end of the rod and gave Cara an amused look. "Well, are you going to have another go or not?"

Cara gave a rueful chuckle. "No fooling you, is there, Breena?"

"You'd have to be up pretty early in the morning." Breena checked the position of the moon. "Now I think of it, we are up pretty early in the morning. Come on."

Between them they replaced the rod. Cara remounted Skydancer and once more set him to fly the course.

To begin with, rods and poles flew all over the place. Cara and Breena, with laborious patience, would replace these and Cara would try again. Skydancer found the hoops particularly difficult. He wasn't used to tucking his wings in, something a dragon never did unless stooping—diving vertically and at great speed to take its prey unawares. He'd given his wings some painful raps before he got the hang of it. He also missed wands in the slalom—the fast wing tip-to-wing tip jinking wasn't natural flying for a dragon, and it was certainly a maneuver Sky had never attempted before. But Cara was a patient teacher and Skydancer a quick learner. He was also brave and nimble, and at length, with Cara practically drooping in the saddle, she and Sky flew a triumphant clear round.

Cara brought Sky in to land, and she and Breena held hands, dancing around in celebration, until there was a sudden, shocking beat of powerful wings overhead, and a carrying voice cried out, "Who's there?"

Startled, Cara, Breena, and Sky drew back into the shadows.

"What is it?" another voice called.

Breena put her mouth close to Cara's ear and whispered, "That's Galen's voice—it must be the guard flight. They should have come in hours ago."

"I could have sworn I saw someone flying around the practice ring." A dragon swooped closer. Just at that moment, to the great relief of Cara and Breena, a cloud covered the moon.

"You're seeing things, Mellan," cried Galen's voice. "Why would anyone in their right mind be flying round the show ring at this hour of the morning?"

"I tell you, I saw—"

"A night bird, most like. We've already hunted a phantom pack of firedogs you think you saw halfway across Seahaven."

Mellan's voice was sulky. "I could have sworn . . ."

"Never mind, lad. But let's not start any more pertyons, eh? I'm fairly pining for my nice warm bed."

A few moments later, the sound of wing beats faded and Cara and Breena remembered to breathe.

"Hah." Breena's voice was scornful. "Men are such idiots! When I make the guard flight, if I see something fishy going on, I'll investigate it no matter what Galen says."

"Just as well you're not flying with them, then," said Cara. She shuddered. "That was close."

"It was." Breena's voice was troubled. "You're flying very near the storm, Cara."

"I know," said Cara. In the shadow, Breena couldn't see her face, which was probably just as well. "But I can't stop now."

Cara resisted riding Sky the next day, but was up early the following morning. Once her father had set off with the first string of racing dragons, she and Sky headed for the shepherd's hut.

As she tacked up Sky, he clawed at the ground eagerly. "You'd better be on your best behavior today," Cara told him. "I'm going to undo the saddle belt and just use a tether."

Riding without a saddle belt was one of the most dangerous forms of flying a dragon, but it was the ultimate expression of the Trustbond, and essential for riders who wished to develop a feel for their riding rhythm. It was vital that the dragon should fly straight and level; any unexpected twists or turns could catch the rider unawares and throw her out of the saddle. Many riders trying this maneuver for the first time fell off, hence the need for the safety tether.

The two were soon in the air, and Cara urged Sky up and down the valley above the brooding water of the black lake. Once she felt the dragon was warmed up and concentrating, Cara made her decision. "Steady, Sky," she said. "Nice and easy, please."

With a mixture of trepidation and excitement, Cara carefully undid her saddle belt. Only her riding skill would keep her in the saddle now. At first it felt no different from normal riding, but as Sky cut through the air, Cara began to feel the difference. Small, subtle changes in the position of her torso were needed to remain properly balanced yet still be able to steer with the leg reins. Quick, jerky movements caused overcompensation, leading to loss of control. Once or twice Cara felt herself tipping to one side before managing to regain her balance and bring herself back into the saddle. *Like sitting on a tightrope,* she thought.

By the end of the hour, Cara felt more confident. A technique that took most riders months to acquire was coming naturally to her. *Riding is in my blood,* she thought. "Thank you, Ma," she said quietly. She broke into a smile. "And thank you, too, Sky, for being such an incredible dragon! One more pass down the valley, then we go home."

She pulled on the reins to make Sky turn.

"Cara!"

Startled, Cara looked down. Standing on the rim of the valley below was her father and, by his side, Hortense.

Cara's stomach knotted. Her mind blanked as all rational thought disappeared. In her panic, she pulled to her right with the ear reins, but signaled to go left with her leg rein. Sky was caught between two orders. He flipped one way, then the next, desperately trying to obey Cara's instructions.

"Cara!"

Sky banked sharply from
left to right before pulling up
into a steep climb. Cara gave
a cry as the reins slipped
out of her hands. She tried
to thrust her feet deeper
into the stirrup irons, and
scrabbled to grab hold of the
saddle handgrip, but Sky's
sudden
swerve
caused her to tip
sideways. She swayed
in the saddle. Her feet were
sliding out of the ill-fitting
stirrup irons. A single thought
pulsed in her mind: *I'm tethered,
I'm tethered!* The safety line

would hold her, dangling
ignominiously, until Sky could
let her down to the ground.
Desperately she tried to
regain her balance, but it was
impossible. Gravity took her in
an irresistible grip and she toppled
out of the saddle.

Her headlong fall ended with
a jerk as the tether snapped taut.
Her head was buffeted
against the dragon's
side as she was tossed
about like a rag doll.

It's all right, I'm tethered! she
thought, her hand instinctively reaching up
for the leather strap. As she did so, she gave a
gasp of horror. The stitching holding the clip to
the tether was ripping open. "Sky, land!" she
screamed. "Land now!"

The dragon seemed not to hear. He banked steeply and increased his speed.

"No, Sky, no!"

Then the leather snapped. Cara screamed again as she hurtled earthward. She braced herself for the bone-splitting impact. It didn't happen; she felt a jarring that drove the breath from her body. Then she seemed to drop into a hole of her own making, into a black silence. Cold, wet, suffocating fingers of water thrust into her ears and nostrils. She had fallen into the lake.

Under the frothing surface Cara struggled desperately. The remains of the tether had wrapped around her arms, trapping them to her sides. Cara kicked furiously and her head burst out from the inky waters. Instinctively, she took in what air she could, before plunging back into the depths.

Cara kicked out again and again, desperately trying to free her arms. It was no use. She was tied fast. She felt her strength, and her consciousness, slipping away.

Then there was a blaze of light and a cacophony of noise. Bands of iron tightened around Cara's chest and she felt herself being lifted from the dark, clutching water. As she broke the surface, she sucked in great lungfuls of air, dimly aware of the talons that held her fast, the great wings that were carrying her to safety, and Sky's concerned face peering anxiously into her own.

Before she knew it, she was lying on the grass at the side of the lake, with Sky standing over her, hooting with alarm and distress.

Cara sat up, coughing and spluttering, and gazed at the worried dragon with gratitude and wonder. Sky hadn't disobeyed her for no reason—he must have known that he couldn't land in time, and that Cara's only chance was to fall into water rather than onto the unrelenting rocks of the valley floor.

"Cara!"

There was no more time for thought; Cara's father was upon them. He was shaking, his fists clenched into white balls. Cara had never seen him in such a fury. Behind him stood Hortense. She was smiling.

Cara felt helpless. "I'm all right, Da." She struggled to her feet, attempting to reassure her father. "I'm not hurt. Sky saved me—" She broke off, knowing there was no point in trying to defend the indefensible.

When her father finally spoke, there was no admonishment, just a statement of fact. "You disobeyed my wishes, but worse still, you lied to me."

It made Cara feel even more wretched.

"How long have you been riding this dragon?" continued Huw. "And do not lie to me, Cara, not again."

And so the story came out. In her shame and guilt, Cara told her father about everything: the warning from Drane, the attack of the firedogs and howlers, and all that she had done since. The confession was made worse for Cara not by her father's silence, nor by his stone-set face, but by the fact that she had to tell it all in the presence of Hortense, who was clearly reveling in her discomfort.

When Cara finished, her father remained silent for some moments before taking a deep breath. "Cara, I have already lost someone I loved very dearly, and I nearly lost you today. It will not happen again, do you understand?"

Cara nodded.

"As for Skydancer, he will be sold." He held up a hand to cut off Cara's protest. "I warned you last time. I say, he will be sold. To anyone who will take such a beast," he added.

"I'll take him," said Hortense. "If he can be tamed . . . ," she added.

"No!" cried Cara. "You can't!"

A flood of anger finally burst Huw's dam of self-control. "I will not be questioned!" he roared. "It seems that you have managed to ride him, so he is no longer the wild beast I thought he was. You will make him accept Hortense as a rider. If not, I will sell him for a watch-dragon!"

Cara shook her head, tears in her eyes. "No, Da, no."

"That is my decision. You have to make yours."

*   *   *

Huw led the subdued Skydancer up the hill. Cara caught up with Hortense, who was following several paces behind the Dragonmaster. "You told my father," she said in a low voice. It wasn't a question. "How did you know where we were?"

Hortense gave a little smile. "My father keeps hunting dragons, had you forgotten? I had his best tracker follow you. I knew exactly where you'd be."

Cara said nothing. If she attacked Hortense again, she knew it would not be forgiven.

The little party breasted the hill to find two waiting dragons. Huw took the reins of one and turned to Cara. "You will lead Skydancer back to Dragonsdale—on foot the whole way. Do not even think of flying—patrols will be out keeping watch."

With these words, Huw stepped onto his dragon's raised foreleg, vaulted into the saddle, and took to the air. Hortense gave Cara a triumphant smirk and followed on the other dragon.

Cara had plenty of time to think on the long, footsore journey. All the way home she brooded on what the future held for her, and for Sky.

If she didn't give Sky up, her father would certainly be true to his word. He would clip Sky's wings, and sell him as a lowly watch-dragon, like the pathetic beast that prowled the Dragonsdale stable yard at night, slinking listlessly around on the hard cobbles, yearning for the freedom of the air that it would never know again. For if a dragon couldn't fly, what was the point of its existence? It was an elemental creature of earth, fire, and air.

Cara could never allow Sky to become a watch-dragon! It was a fate usually reserved for beasts too old and frail to fly—or, as a last resort, for unmanageable dragons. Her heart sank at the thought of her darling Sky spending his days chained to a gatepost to deter unwanted strangers. It would be a fate worse than death, and she had to prevent it. Whatever it took.

Wony, Drane, and Breena were waiting as Cara and Skydancer limped into the stable yard. They had seen the arrival of Hortense and the Dragonmaster, and had heard the orders he had given Galen to watch over Cara's return. They had instantly known that the game was up.

Breena gave Cara a hug. Wony blinked away tears. Drane appeared to be about to say something, but he closed his mouth hurriedly and scuttled away as Huw emerged from Dragonsdale House. He had no wish to be questioned by the Dragonmaster about the depth of his involvement in Cara's deception. Huw glowered at Breena and Wony until they, too, seemed to remember that they had urgent unfinished business elsewhere.

In Dragonsdale House, Gerda looked down from a bedroom window as Cara and the Dragonmaster were left alone in the stable yard. She shook her head sadly. "The poor mite," she whispered.

Huw regarded Cara with a stony stare. "Well, daughter?"

Cara's lips quivered. "I'm sorry, Da, I wanted you to be proud of me. I wanted to be like Ma."

Her father's grim face was unrelenting.

Cara continued. "I'm sorry for what I did, for deceiving you. And I shouldn't have lied to you. But it's done and I can't go back and undo what's happened." She paused and drew breath. "But I wouldn't change my time flying with Sky. I wouldn't swap that for anything in the Isles. I'm sorry, Da, but I don't want to lie to you ever again, and that's the truth of it."

"And what of the dragon?"

Cara closed her eyes and bowed her head. Biting her lip, she managed to fight back a sob. "Hortense shall have him."

There was a silence.

"Very well," said Huw at length. "I will make arrangements with Lord Torin."

Cara's mind was in a turmoil of agony and misery, but one thing was clear to her: She could think of only one way in which Sky might be persuaded to accept Hortense. "May I say good-bye to Sky?"

"You may." The Dragonmaster nodded, and went back into the house.

Cara took Sky back to his stable. Once inside, she slammed the door and turned a scowling face on the dragon. "You stupid beast!" she shouted. She struck his side. "You're so stubborn and proud! First you think you're too good to let yourself be ridden. And when I do ride you, what happens? You let me fall! You were supposed to fly straight, and you didn't. I could have been killed! I never want to ride you again!"

Sky shuffled back, confused.

"Well, that's it, I've finished with you! You're Hortense's now. Try your high-and-mighty ways with her and you'll be beaten! And if you don't do what she tells you, you'll have your wings clipped—and that's what you deserve."

Hooting and crying in distress, Sky backed away from Cara's attack.

"It's all your own fault. You stupid, stubborn creature! I don't want to see you ever again!" Cara stormed out of the stable, slamming the door shut behind her once again and cutting off Sky's desperate calls.

She marched fiercely across the yard. Wony, peering around the door of the tack room, made as if to follow her, but Breena caught the younger girl by the arm and shook her head.

When she reached the back of the stable block, away

from prying eyes, Cara's fierce self-possession left her. She fell to her knees, tears streaming down her face, great gulping sobs racking her body. She cried for her father, for her mother, for herself, for Sky, and for the bright future that she had glimpsed for a moment, but which now would never be.

FAREWELL
TO SKY

A few days later, Lord Torin stood in the stable yard in his usual stance—splayfooted, with his fingers stuck in the belt whose main function seemed to be to prevent his sizable paunch from slipping any further. A look of disapproval was etched into his florid face as he watched Skydancer being brought from the stable. Hortense stood at his side, dressed for riding, her face set in an insufferable smirk.

In order to separate Sky from Cara, Huw had offered him to Lord Torin for a price that the notoriously tightfisted High Lord would find difficult to refuse, but only on condition that Skydancer be kept at Torin's own stables. Lord Torin was caught between his desire for a bargain and doubts about allowing his precious daughter to ride a dangerously temperamental dragon.

"Not at all sure about this, Dragonmaster," the High Lord said gruffly. "Been having second thoughts, isn't it? Whuff! Once bitten, twice shy."

Huw raised his hand in preparation to order that

Skydancer be returned to his stall. "If Your Lordship would rather Hortense did not—"

"Nonsense, Father! I can ride Skydancer," said Hortense in a voice that made Cara squirm. "What happened last time was all because they hadn't prepared him properly. He knows what'll happen to him if he misbehaves this time . . ." She flashed Cara a look of gloating triumph. "Doesn't he, Cara?"

Cara bowed her head and said nothing. Mistress Hildebrand pursed her lips in disapproval. Breena, who had no business to be amongst those present at all, put an arm around Cara's shoulders and directed a look of pure loathing at Hortense.

Lord Torin pursed his lips and studied the dragon. "Well, I must say, Dragonmaster, he looks as if you've thrashed some of the wickedness out of him."

Skydancer did, indeed, look like a very miserable, spiritless dragon. His tail dragged along the ground, his ears drooped, his head hung low, his eyes were dull, and he moved around the stable yard as though he felt that walking was simply not worth the effort. He kept giving Cara plaintive sidelong glances, which she resolutely ignored.

Huw glared at the High Lord. "I assure you, Lord Torin, that this dragon has not been ill-treated in any way."

Torin dismissed this with a wave. "Whuff! Well, let's see how he does on the rein first."

The Dragonmaster led the way out of the stable yard into the meadow beyond, and stood conversing with Lord Torin in a low voice while Bran and a couple of stable hands harnessed the docile dragon for the long reins to his shoulder and thigh. Huw himself took control and flicked the shoulder rein, signaling Skydancer to begin. The dragon took off and flew in a circle with the Dragonmaster at its center, responding to his signals to fly higher or lower immediately and without complaint.

"Hmmm. Whuff!" said Torin, scratching his chin. "Well, he seems quiet enough."

Cara watched Skydancer's slow, obedient circuits through eyes that seemed filled with mist. *Yes,* she thought, *because he thinks I hate him. He doesn't care anymore.*

Huw completed the exercise and handed the reins to one of the senior Dragonsdale riders. Mistress Hildebrand watched closely as Skydancer flew an obedience exercise. She nodded as dragon and rider executed a faultless figure eight and a slow glide into a hover. "Not bad," she said. "Not bad at all." She glanced at Cara, who stood next to her watching Skydancer fly with an expression of inconsolable loss. "Now that he's finally made up his mind to behave, that dragon of yours is making good progress."

"He's not my dragon," said Cara tightly. "He's going to be Hortense's."

"Ah, yes," said Mistress Hildebrand, turning back to watch the next part of the exercise. "I was forgetting. Whomever he belongs to, I have to admit that he seems to know what he's doing."

"That would be because Cara taught him how." Breena tossed her head angrily. She had been furious on Cara's behalf ever since the decision to sell Sky had become known. "Just because the Dragonmaster won't let her fly," she continued, "it doesn't mean she doesn't know how to!"

Mistress Hildebrand gave Breena a frosty glance. "Less of your impudence, miss. Riders at this stable do not concern themselves about which dragons are bought and sold, or about who gets to fly and who does not."

"Well, maybe they should, so!" Breena snapped back, unabashed. "Maybe if they did, we wouldn't have a good rider and a good dragon both eating their hearts out, and no one benefiting at all but that polecat Hortense, for shame." Turning, she saw that the Dragonmaster was no great distance away—certainly close enough to hear Breena's comments, which had not been uttered quietly.

But instead of curling up with embarrassment, she strode off, her back as stiff as a board, eloquently radiating disapproval from every inch of her frame.

Huw gave no sign of having heard Breena's outburst. He walked across the grass to where Torin and Hortense were standing. "Well, my lord," he said, "do you wish your daughter to ride this dragon?"

The High Lord dithered for a moment. Then he caught Hortense's glare and gave an impatient shrug. "My life won't be worth living if she doesn't. Whuff! Very well."

Saddle and riding reins were brought, and Sky allowed

himself to be harnessed and led to the mounting block. At length, the hands stood back. Hortense gave Cara a last victorious smirk, then strode across the short grass, swinging her whip. As she paused before mounting, she brandished the whip in Sky's face and said, quite audibly, "If you mess about with me, you stupid creature, you'll feel this hot and strong."

Sky gave her a look of undisguised contempt. Then the momentary spark in his eye faded, and he turned his head to stare into the distance. He waited, resigned, listless, as if he had put away everything that made him the dragon he was into some private corner of his being, remote and unreachable.

Cara never took her eyes off Skydancer. She felt as though her heart were being squeezed in ice-cold hands. *I won't cry,* she thought. *I won't give Hortense the satisfaction.* Hortense climbed the mounting block, put her foot into a stirrup iron, and swung herself up into the saddle. She fastened the safety belt and tether. Then she dug her heels into the dragon's flanks and hauled on the ear reins with quite unnecessary force. Sky gave no sign of resenting the vicious tug: He obediently rose into the air.

For half an hour Hortense put Sky through his paces. Her sessions with Huw had improved her riding skills somewhat; nevertheless, she managed to give enough confusing signals to keep Sky off balance, and berated him roundly with voice, hands, boots, and whip whenever he failed to respond as she wished. Cara watched this display of ignorance, injustice, and willful callousness with mounting indignation. She felt sick and furious. But she said nothing. There was nothing to say.

Hortense brought Sky in to land, dismounted, and tossed his reins to Bran. She strode across to her father and folded her arms.

Torin rubbed his chin. "I don't know, Dragonmaster. I mean, this is all well and good—but I've seen what this beast can do when he's roused—eh? Whuff! How can I be sure he hasn't still got the devil in him? Tell me that."

"Please, Father," said Hortense in her sweetest voice. Cara winced. Hortense being reasonable was, for some reason, even more hateful than Hortense being her usual arrogant self. "Skydancer is a valuable dragon—you said so yourself. Goldenbrows are very rare. And Master Huw is offering him at a very reasonable price."

"Hmmm." This was true. In order to get rid of Skydancer, and as a gesture of goodwill toward Lord Torin, Huw had offered to let Sky go for a fraction of his real worth. The High Lord couldn't have bought even a watch-dragon so cheaply. "But what if he turns out to be no good in the arena after all?" demanded Torin petulantly. "Waste of good money, isn't it? Whuff!"

"Well, as to that . . ." Hortense was speaking to her father, but her eyes were on Cara. "As to that," she repeated, "surely it's worth the gamble? He's much stronger and quicker than Valeweaver. I'm sure he'll give me the edge in the Island Championships."

Huw gave her a stern look. "You have not qualified for the championships."

"Oh, hadn't you heard?" said Hortense blithely. "One of the qualifiers has been taken ill. I'm entered on a wild card."

Cara was willing to bet that the wild-card entry had been arranged by Lord Torin; she wouldn't have put it past him to arrange the unfortunate competitor's "illness," too.

"In any case," Hortense told her father, "if Skydancer does well, you have a bargain. And if not—you can always cut your losses." Cara gasped. Could Hortense really be suggesting . . . ? "After all," Hortense concluded calmly, "there's no point in keeping a useless dragon."

Cara felt her throat tighten. She suddenly found it difficult to breathe. There it was—Hortense's revenge. If Sky didn't obey her, he would be destroyed.

Lord Torin gave Huw a lofty glance. "Very well, Dragonmaster," he said, with the air of one conferring a great favor. "I'll take the beast off your hands at the agreed price. Have him ready for the day after tomorrow." He nodded to Huw, who bowed stiffly in return, and waddled away to his waiting calash. Hortense, with one last gloating look at Cara, followed.

"Cara," said Huw, "go and lend a hand in the tack room, will you?"

Cara nodded, and went off without a word or a backward glance.

The Dragonmaster signaled Bran to take Skydancer back to his stable. He turned to face Mistress Hildebrand. "I suppose you disapprove of what I've done as well."

The Chief Riding Instructor gave him a look in which exasperation was finely mixed with sympathy. "That's not for me to say. It's no business of mine."

"That's never stopped you before," growled Huw. After a pause, he went on. "Maybe I was overly hasty to offer the beast to Torin. But I will not have Cara ride, and as long as that wretched dragon is here, I see no way of stopping her. Once Skydancer is gone, I hope she won't want to ride another dragon — at least, not so much that she'd disobey me to do so."

"That's not . . . kind," said Mistress Hildebrand.

Huw rubbed his eyes. "Nobody said it was."

"And you will not change your mind? You will never let her ride?"

"I cannot." Huw's voice was thick with his old grief. "You know I cannot."

"Then, perhaps," said Mistress Hildebrand, almost gently, "this way is the best."

"It is," said the Dragonmaster wearily. "I'm sure it is. In any case, the bargain is made and there is no going back. I just wish Cara did not mind it so."

The morning Skydancer left Dragonsdale, there was an unusual number of people on the farm, apparently with time on their hands, gathered in the meadow behind the stable.

It was a long way to Lord Torin's manor on the other side of the Island. Autumn was upon them with its chill winds, and the day was unusually cold for the time of year. Hortense had sent her head groom to fly Skydancer to his new home. Kern was an uncouth, bad-tempered man with a cast in one eye, who had been dismissed from several dragon farms for treating dragons cruelly.

Cara was surrounded by her friends. Wony was

crying. Breena was glaring at Kern as if, by doing so, she hoped to burn him to ashes where he stood. Drane looked angry and miserable. Gerda had one arm around Cara; with the other, she held a corner of her shawl to her face. Mistress Hildebrand stood to one side, wringing her riding gloves in her hands as though wishing they were Kern's ample neck.

The Dragonmaster handed Skydancer's reins to Kern. "There you are," he said. "Lord Torin will find that he has been fully prepared."

"He'd better have been," rasped the groom. "If not . . ." He held up a villainous-looking whip. "If not, he'll have a taste of this before he's much older."

"There'll be no need for that." Cara stepped forward. With all her heart, she longed to run to Skydancer, fling her arms around him, tell him how much she loved him—but she knew she could not. She was perfectly in control of herself.

She stood facing Skydancer. For a moment, the dragon looked up with desperate hope. "Good-bye, Skydancer," said Cara in a perfectly level voice. "Do as Hortense tells you. I shan't see you again."

She turned and walked away. Sky gave a single hoot of distress, then lowered his head to wait, submissively, for whatever fate now held in store for him.

Kern climbed into the saddle, touched his hat offhandedly to the Dragonmaster, and pulled back on the reins. Sky took off. None of the onlookers moved. They watched as Sky flew away, growing smaller and smaller: now no more than a dot in the great vault of the sky, now lost to view altogether.

No one spoke. Gerda gave a muffled sob. Wony wept bitterly.

Cara turned and walked back to the stable yard. The crowd parted. No one tried to stop her.

Cara sat on the still-warm pumice bed in Skydancer's stable and ran the dragon's discarded noseband through her fingers again and again, staring at nothing, filled with a grief that was too deep even for tears.

THE ISLAND CHAMPIONSHIPS

The day of the Island Championships had arrived.

Cara sat glumly on the lumbering oxcart as it breasted the last hill on the road. There, laid out before her, were the show arena, where the competition was to be held, the mushroom forest of tents between it and the neat town of South Landing, and the glint of the sea beyond.

The journey from Dragonsdale on the baggage cart had taken three days. The cart had rattled and grumbled its way along the unpaved road, its wheels sticking in ruts and muddy valley bottoms.

Every rider and available hand from Dragonsdale was to be at the championships, lending their support to Breena and the other dragonriders competing in the senior events. Cara was riding the cart because Huw had rigidly enforced his ban on her flying to the championships, even in a calash. Wony and Drane had volunteered to accompany her and the two carters on the journey.

At other times in her life, Cara would have enjoyed the overnight stops, with their smells of wood smoke and hot

stew, the quiet talk and companionable laughter as she lay near the fire tucked up in her bedroll. She would have been content to gaze up at the stars and the occasional appearances of Galen's patrol wing as it swept overhead, checking that their surroundings were free from danger. But since Sky's departure, she had withdrawn into herself, replying to Wony's and Drane's halting attempts at conversation with perfect politeness but no enthusiasm whatsoever, so that in the end they left her alone, almost afraid of their silent, distant friend.

The cart descended the hill and rolled along the roadway between the tents, easing its way through the crowds. It seemed that the entire population of Seahaven had turned out to watch the championships: The sky above was filled with dragons wheeling and coming in to land, while stable hands from every dragon farm on the Island were waiting to take the reins from their riders and lead the dragons to picket lines.

Bran came to meet the cart and give Drane and Wony instructions for unloading. "Cara," he said, "go and help Breena—she'll be called for her event soon." Cara nodded and made her way through the crowds to the show arena.

As she went through the gates into the arena, Cara looked around for familiar faces. She recognized some of the riders from showings at Dragonsdale; many more were unknown to her. But Hortense was not there, and nor, to Cara's mixed relief and disappointment, was Sky.

The competitors who were to fly later were studying the obstacles, learning the flight paths they would have to negotiate later in the day. Cara gazed up at the course with intense interest. The brightly painted rods and hoops hanging far above her were suspended from masts, which towered half as high again as the ones at Dragonsdale. The obstacles were better made than the ones at home, and much more highly decorated. They seemed bigger, too, though Cara realized that this must be an illusion. Bigger obstacles would be easier to negotiate. But there were more of them, and some of them were very impressive.

Cara looked up beyond the masts, and stifled a gasp of wonderment. The vertical poles—two sets of them—were suspended beneath tethered balloons. Cara had seen pictures of such devices but had never seen one in reality. They were huge, and gloriously patterned in crimson and gold. A large wicker basket hung beneath each. As Cara stared, spellbound, a green head appeared above the basket rim of the furthermost balloon and, with a *whumph!* a jet of flame appeared, playing into the opening at the base of the canopy. The balloon rose very slightly, straining against its moorings. Cara realized that there was a watch-dragon in the basket, flaming to produce the hot air needed to give lift.

In the center of the arena was a tall tower made of wood with canvas sides, painted, like the balloons, in crimson and gold. This was where the judges would stand, where they would have an uninterrupted view of the whole course and every obstacle. There was a wooden bridge leading from the stands to the tower, high and wide enough for a dragon to fly beneath—a formidable obstacle.

Cara found Breena dressed in working clothes and gazing apprehensively at the final obstacle of the course—a fearsome triple under 'n' over. This was a set of three rods set close together across a dragon's line of flight. Dragon and rider would have to fly under the first rod, over the second rod, which was set

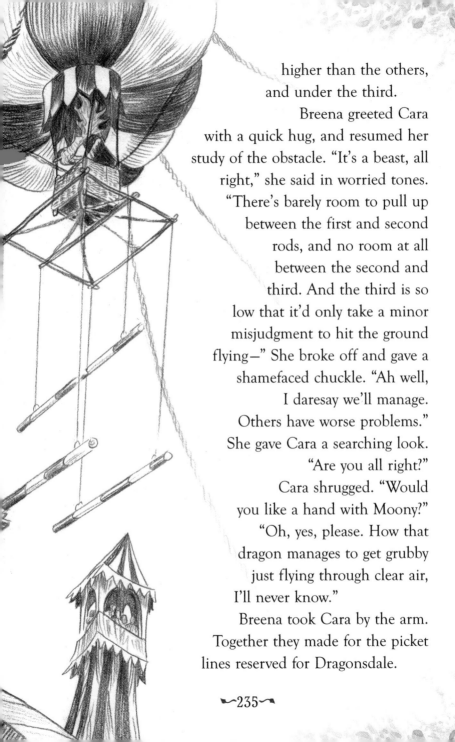

higher than the others, and under the third.

Breena greeted Cara with a quick hug, and resumed her study of the obstacle. "It's a beast, all right," she said in worried tones. "There's barely room to pull up between the first and second rods, and no room at all between the second and third. And the third is so low that it'd only take a minor misjudgment to hit the ground flying—" She broke off and gave a shamefaced chuckle. "Ah well, I daresay we'll manage. Others have worse problems." She gave Cara a searching look. "Are you all right?"

Cara shrugged. "Would you like a hand with Moony?"

"Oh, yes, please. How that dragon manages to get grubby just flying through clear air, I'll never know."

Breena took Cara by the arm. Together they made for the picket lines reserved for Dragonsdale.

"Is Hortense here yet?" asked Cara, keeping her voice steady with an effort.

Breena grimaced. "Oh, yes, Her Ladyship's here." She stopped and turned to face Cara. "In fact, she's got the stall next to mine. I don't even know why she's billeted on us, considering she hasn't set foot in Dragonsdale since—" Breena broke off. "Not that I'm complaining about that," she went on hurriedly. "The less I see of Hortense, the better I like it. But I don't see why we should put up with her just because her father's too mean to pay for his own space in the lines."

"It doesn't matter," said Cara in a colorless voice. She set off for the line of temporary stalls. Breena regarded her for a moment or two with anxiety, then followed.

Cara heard Hortense before she saw her. "Oh, yes," she was telling a group of cackling cronies, "as you see, I managed to tame the so-called untamable dragon."

Cara steeled herself to peer into the stall where Hortense was holding court. Hortense's friends were simpering at her and making faces at a dragon that Cara recognized only with difficulty.

Although he had been prepared for the competition with the utmost care (though not by Hortense, if Cara knew anything about it), Skydancer was clearly an unhappy dragon. His scales shone, but his eyes were dull and lusterless, and his whole carriage was listless, disillusioned, withdrawn from his surroundings, slumped in defeat.

Sky was clearly pining. He gazed at Hortense without love, without even hate, simply with dull indifference. His spirit, if not broken, seemed to be so battered that he could not be bothered to fight anymore to preserve his freedom.

For a moment, Sky looked up and saw Cara. A light was rekindled in his great dark eyes, and he gave a beseeching grunt. Cara longed to go to him and embrace him, but she caught Hortense's cold, knowing look and reminded herself what the consequences might be. She turned her back on Sky and walked on. Sky's head drooped, and the light faded from his eyes.

For the next hour or so, Cara helped Breena to prepare Moonflight. In the neighboring stall, Hortense's braying friends continued to gush their congratulations on her feat in taming the rogue dragon, and to assure her that she would wipe the floor with her rivals, that the championship was in the bag, that the cup had her name on it already. Breena muttered darkly under her breath as she polished Moonflight's scales. Wony and Drane looked in from time to time, unhappily aware that there was little they could do to help Breena or Cara with their respective struggles, but feeling honor bound to offer what support they could.

When the bell rang to signal the start of flying, Cara joined Drane and Wony in the stands. She spotted her father and Mistress Hildebrand sitting beside

Lord Torin in the owners' and trainers' area, and quickly looked away.

The championship program began with flying displays. These were always enjoyed by the crowd. Formation flying was not a competition event, and there was no prize to be won; nevertheless, every dragon farm took its display very seriously—as did the few wealthy owners like Lord Torin who could afford to keep a display team. The knowledgeable spectators would decide for themselves which team had given the best display, and their decision would confer great, if unofficial, prestige upon the successful farm or owner.

Cara tried to be interested as the dragons soared overhead, flying wing tip to wing tip, with streamers in their stable colors flowing behind them, performing turns, loops, rolls, and figure eights in perfect unison before changing their formation, often in the middle of a roll or turn: diamond, arrow, swan, eagle. To her eyes—and, from conversations she overheard between her neighbors in the stands, to many others as well— Dragonsdale's team gave the most faultless display, but other voices were raised in support of the Clapperclaw team, whose flashy low flying was certainly exciting, even if its formations were generally ragged.

After the formation displays, there was a lull in the proceedings. Breena slipped away to change her clothes and lead Moonflight into the ring for the Best Presented competition. As there was no Beginners and Novices class in the Island Championships, this would be followed into the ring by the Intermediate Clear Flight.

Drane bought Wony and Cara wild boar pasties for lunch. Cara thanked him, but she only nibbled at a corner of the pasty before secretly feeding the rest to one of the many hounds that always seemed to be present at a dragon showing, shamelessly scrounging tidbits and leftovers from all and sundry.

The judges' careful examination of the dragons offered for the Best Presented prize was lost on Cara. She only had eyes for Sky. Despite his immaculate turnout, it was obvious that no one could possibly award a prize to such a spiritless beast, even a Goldenbrow, and Sky was passed over, much to Hortense's annoyance.

Cara clapped dutifully as the results were announced, and was genuinely pleased when Breena and Moonflight took the blue rosette for second place. But her momentary elation died as quickly as it had arisen. Suddenly she could not bear to remain in the stands, a mere spectator. Muttering an excuse to Drane and Wony, she left her seat and slipped into the competitors' enclosure, where Breena was anxiously watching the first dragon attempt the course.

She took Cara's arm without speaking, and her eyes barely flickered from the first competitors performing a tight knife-edge turn around a pylon. Along with all the spectators, Breena gasped as the dragon swept under the bridge, scant inches from the ground, and held her breath as it negotiated the following sets of obstacles before weaving in and out of the slalom wands. The dragon was an agile beast and its rider clearly knew what she was doing. Nevertheless, the pair had collected twenty penalty points by the time they came to the final obstacle.

Breena's grip on Cara's arm tightened as the dragon flew low and slipped under the first rod. It climbed steeply, beating its great wings with a force that amounted almost to desperation. Barely clearing the second rod, it went into a dive . . . and took the third rod full on its breast, sending the light wooden beam spinning to the sand of the arena, to a huge groan from the crowd.

Three red flags appeared on top of the tower. Breena turned a worried face to Cara. "Thirty points—and that's good flying, on this course! That last obstacle is a nightmare. Oh, Cara, how am I going to get Moony around without us making fools of ourselves?"

"The way you usually do," said Cara firmly. "You're a good rider and you've got a good dragon. It's the same for all the others."

Breena took a deep breath. "I know, but . . ."

"You're going to win, and rub Ernestina's nose in it, and join the guard flight—and even if you don't, you'll still have flown in the Island Championships." Cara gave Breena an odd little smile. "You're here, with Moony. You won't get many days like this. Enjoy it."

Breena laughed softly. "I thought I was supposed to be the sensible one. You're right. If I can't enjoy myself when I'm riding Moony, what's the point? We're going to go out there and have fun."

Nevertheless, Breena continued to watch her competitors with unwavering concentration, her eyes narrowed and her brow wrinkled in thought. "There's a trick to that last obstacle," she muttered. "Nobody's cleared it yet. I don't think it can be cleared by flying in the usual way." Her brow cleared. "Unless . . ." She turned to face Cara, grinning with a wild recklessness that was quite foreign to her usual placid nature. "Cara, I've got an idea. If it works, it'll be the most brilliant idea in the history of dragonflying, I'll win the championship, and Galen will have to let me into the guard flight. But if it doesn't work, I'm going to look like the biggest idiot there ever was."

Cara stared at her friend. "What . . . ?"

But there was no time for inquiries. Breena's number was called, and she gave Cara another wild grin and walked quickly away, leaving her friend puzzled and apprehensive.

Cara hurried to rejoin Wony and Drane in the stands. Wony looked up at her with a troubled expression. "Nobody's got a clear flight yet," she said. "In fact, nobody's scored better than twenty penalties. Do you think Breena . . . ?"

"Don't worry about Breena," said Cara, with more confidence than she felt. "She's got a trick up her sleeve." *I only hope that it works, whatever it is,* she added silently to herself.

The bell rang and Breena began her round. From the first, it was obvious that she had decided to ignore Mistress Hildebrand's years of advice and throw caution to the winds. Her turn around the first balloon was so tight that her helmet almost brushed the canopy, and the watch-dragon in the basket below cowered beneath the rim and folded its clipped wings over its eyes. All her succeeding turns were fast and tight, leaving no margin for error on her approach to the obstacles. But Breena made few errors. On the double horizontal, Moonflight's wing tip did brush a rod, which wobbled alarmingly, but did not fall. With only the final triple to go, so far Breena was clear.

But then something seemed to go wrong. Instead of taking the turn from the final hoop in the same dashing style, Breena could be seen to rein Moonflight in. The dragon's headlong pace slowed until she had barely enough airspeed to maintain level flight.

Wony was standing, unable to remain in her seat. "What's she doing? She's going too slowly! She won't have the speed to get over the top bar!"

But Cara, in a flash of inspiration, understood what Breena was about. "No," she cried, "she's doing it deliberately! She's going to stall!"

Cara was right. Breena slipped Moonflight under the first bar with inches to spare. The dragon climbed laboriously to the top bar . . . slowed . . . and stopped

dead in midair right above it. The crowd gasped. Moonflight seemed to hover motionless above the bar for a long, breathless moment—then she slipped backward a fraction, and put her nose down into a dive.

Wony screamed. Drane leapt to his feet. "They're going to crash!"

The crowd thought so, too: A gasp echoed around the stands. On the arena floor, officials scattered and the surgical team reached for their stretcher.

But at the last moment, Moonflight's downward plunge gave her enough airspeed to generate lift once more, and the dragon soared under the third bar, pulling out of her dive a scale's breadth from the ground, and soared back above the arena to relieved applause.

Wony was bouncing up and down, clapping her hands in glee. "She made it! She flew clear!"

But Cara had spotted an official in the ring, furiously waving a red flag. "I don't think so. Moony must have touched the ground. . . ."

The crowd quieted as others noticed the flag. There was a pause while the official mounted the tower to hold a hurried conference with the judges. Then the hoist on the tower displayed a single red flag.

Wony groaned in disappointment. "Ten penalties!" She turned to Cara. "I don't understand—what was Breena trying to do?"

"She'd worked out that there wasn't enough room between the second and third rods to go from a climb into a dive, so she did a controlled stall. For a dragon's wings to work, the dragon has to be going forward—if it stops, like Breena made Moony do, the wings won't work and it stalls. It's how birds land. But then Moony didn't have enough height to build up speed and get her wings working again, so she touched the ground." Cara shrugged. "It was a good idea, but it didn't quite work. Never mind, it's still the best round of the day."

Wony would not be comforted. "But Ernestina hasn't flown yet. If she goes clear, she's won!"

But Ernestina did not fly clear. She gave her usual immaculate display and, like Breena, had collected no faults until she came to the final obstacle. But though she had evidently decided to try Breena's tactic, her nerve failed her: Instead of stalling above the top bar, she allowed Stormbringer to go into a dive too early. The bar clattered to the ground, and though rider and dragon recovered to fly beneath the last bar, the single red flag appeared on the tower again to announce that Ernestina, too, had collected ten penalties.

Two more competitors copied Breena's tactics and also scored ten penalties. Another, misjudging his dragon's speed, was unable to recover from his dive and plowed into the ground beneath the third rod, fortunately without serious injury to dragon or rider.

And then it was Hortense's turn.

AN UNOFFICIAL ENTRY

Hortense began her round well. Her lessons with Huw had paid off, and even in his current apathetic state, Skydancer was a superb dragon: quick, agile, responsive—and fearless, if only because he no longer cared what happened to him.

Cara watched them fly the first two obstacles with a flood of emotions churning within her, rising to the surface of her mind and bubbling under turn by turn. She felt a desperate, hopeless love for Sky. She was terrified that he would suffer an accident. Cara was consumed with hatred for Hortense, and racked with hot stabbing pangs of envy that it was her bitter rival, not she, who was up there flying Skydancer.

But as Hortense began to make mistakes, the other feelings died away, and Cara was conscious only of a growing fear for Skydancer's safety. It began with the knife-edge turn around the pylon before the bridge. Hortense misjudged her line and turned too tightly, so that instead of flying through the center of the arch, where the space was greatest, Sky found himself heading too far to the right, into the narrow gap where the arch plunged down to the edge of the arena. Spectators sitting beside the bridge screamed and scattered, and Cara leapt up, heart pounding.

By a seeming miracle, Sky changed direction just enough to jink under the solid timber construction, but his left wing tip flicked the bottom corner of the arch, collecting ten penalties but avoiding utter catastrophe.

Nevertheless, the brush with disaster had rattled Hortense. She failed to reach enough speed for Skydancer to climb in the next double, and dislodged the bottom rod of the higher obstacle. She went wide around the pylon and clipped the hoop that followed, collecting another twenty penalties.

This left Sky badly aligned for the vertical poles, and though he managed to negotiate the obstacle without dislodging a rod, he came within a whisker of crashing into the balloon's mooring ropes and tangling himself and Hortense like flies in a web. The watch-dragon in the basket covered his eyes again.

By this time Sky had gained too much height to turn around the following pylon and between the next set of parallels. Finding himself flying directly toward a collision with the rods, and with no room for maneuvering, Sky banked away, refusing the obstacle. This earned another five penalties, and a furious cut from Hortense's whip as she took Sky back around the pylon to set him at the obstacle again.

The dull indifference that had claimed Cara on Skydancer's departure from Dragonsdale had now completely left her, to be replaced with furious, burning anger. Her fists tightened. How dare Hortense take a whip to Sky when her stupidity had just nearly killed both of them? How could she fly so badly that she made the best dragon in Bresal look like a broken-winded hireling? And how had she, Cara, allowed this to happen? All around the stands, spectators were laughing and shaking their heads at the display of ineptitude in the arena. Cara's eyes blazed. Drane and Wony eyed her with apprehension.

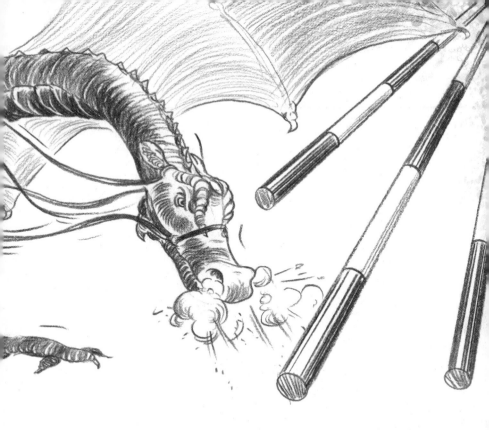

Sky's torment did not last much longer. After collecting another twenty penalties in the slalom, Hortense, in her anxiety to tackle the triple and finish the course, completely missed the preceding hoop. The bell rang to signal her disqualification.

Wony sighed with relief. "Thank goodness for that! I hate to think what would've happened if she'd tried to fly that last triple."

Cara remained tight-lipped, staring at Hortense with loathing.

Her face set in a scowl of disappointed fury, Hortense

neglected to salute the judges in the tower. She turned Skydancer to glide from the ring. Before she had even left the arena, Cara was out of her seat, pushing heedlessly past startled and annoyed spectators. Drane and Wony exchanged worried looks, and followed.

The bell rang for the last competitor to begin her round just as Cara passed through the gate into the small and now deserted enclosure where competitors had awaited their turn in the ring. Hortense had dismounted. She now stood facing Sky, beside herself with rage, brandishing her whip in the dragon's face.

"You useless beast!" she ranted. "You're just as pathetic as all the others! You've made me look like a fool in front of everybody. I'll show you!" She raised her whip and delivered a vicious cut to Skydancer's muzzle.

For a moment, the dragon stared at his rider in shock. Then a burning glow kindled in Skydancer's eyes. He gave a hiss of fury and reared up, spreading his wings in threat. His nostrils dilated, he took a deep breath, and . . .

Hortense's mouth dropped open, her eyes widening in horror as she realized what the dragon

was about to do. Skydancer had been goaded beyond endurance. Now he would fight back in the only way he knew how. Hortense had broken the Trustbond, and nothing remained to deter Sky from following the instincts of his wild ancestors. He was about to flame Hortense to ashes. "Sky! No!"

As the dragon thrust its head forward to strike, Cara threw herself in front of Hortense, facing Sky, her arms spread in mute appeal. Sky blinked—and, at the last moment, turned his head. His fire washed harmlessly over the grass of the enclosure, reducing a considerable part of it to blackened, charred earth.

Hortense was shaking uncontrollably. She could barely speak. "He was going to . . . he would have . . ."

"Yes! And you'd have deserved it!" Cara fought to master her own trembling, and glanced around. The whole incident, though it had seemed to happen in slow motion, had been over in seconds. Every eye in the show arena was trained on the flight of the last competitor. There seemed to be no witnesses except for Drane and Wony, who were stumbling over the grass toward them with shocked expressions.

Hortense was now weeping, overcome with reaction. "He is evil! I'll have him destroyed—"

"Oh, shut up!" Cara turned her back on Hortense and grasped Skydancer's head harness with both hands. She rested her forehead against the golden blaze on Skydancer's brows. The dragon's eyes shone with tenderness and he crooned a greeting. "Sky," Cara said fiercely, "I'm sorry I let you go. I do love you. You're not a useless dragon and we're going to prove it. Right now. Together. Are you ready?" Sky gave a joyful warble. "Come on, then. Let's show them all how it's done."

In the arena, the last competitor had finished her undistinguished round. The crowd was settling to relax and gossip before the fly-off between Breena, Ernestina, and the other two riders who had collected only ten penalties. Officials were strolling toward one another for a cozy chat, while the riggers were casually replacing the rods and poles dislodged during the last flight.

In the stands, Lord Torin gave Huw a sour look. "Hmmmpf! Seems that dragon of yours wasn't all you cracked him up to be, Dragonmaster." Huw said nothing. "Looks as if I'll have to put him to work as a watch-dragon after all. Whuff! One consolation—at least m'daughter didn't have to fly him at that last whatchamacallit. What sort of fool designs an obstacle that's impossible to fly? Hmmm? Whuff!"

Mistress Hildebrand gave him a look of undisguised contempt. Huw's reply was quiet, and he seemed to be speaking more to himself than to the High Lord of Seahaven. "Not impossible, I think," he said. "There is one way of flying it that no one has thought of —"

He broke off as, without warning, the officials who had gathered to chat in the entrance threw themselves onto the sand, as a dragon shot above their heads and burst into the arena.

Lord Torin gawped. "What in the Islands . . . ?" Spectators exchanged baffled glances and checked their programs. A buzz of conversation arose.

Recognizing the dragon, and its rider, Huw surged to his feet. "Cara!"

"That's m'daughter's dragon!" cried Lord Torin, eyes bulging. "Do something, Dragonmaster!"

"I'll get them to ring the bell and stop the round!"

Mistress Hildebrand shook her head. "I don't think a bell is going to stop Cara now."

Huw stared at the dragon and his rider, his mouth working, his eyes full of anguish.

Cara was oblivious to the effect she was creating. She was not dressed for riding: The borrowed safety harness sat oddly over her embroidered jerkin, her skirt was stretched across Skydancer's shoulders, and the helmet she wore (Hortense's spare, commandeered by Drane despite vigorous protests from its owner) was too small for her. But the uneasy chuckles from the crowd died away as she bowed solemnly to the judges and wheeled Sky away to begin her round.

Their Trustbond was reestablished. At once, Cara fell into the easy rhythm she had developed with Sky, their understanding returning in an instant. Most dragons would have needed guiding around the course, even though they had flown it already, but Sky needed no such prompting. He knew where to go. *All I need to do,* thought Cara, *is to make a few suggestions — and not fall off.*

Sky soared toward the first set of vertical poles, tilting his wings sharply to pass between them in a movement almost too swift to follow. The watch-dragon, peering over its basket above, gave a hoot of appreciation. Sky leveled off and dipped into a shallow dive to pick up speed before the first hoop. He tucked in his wings and shot through with ease, to an appreciative murmur from the crowd.

Cara flew Sky around the first pylon in a textbook knife-edge turn and sailed under the bridge in a beautiful curved glide before circling the tower, where the judges were already arguing over this irregular development. Sky darted between the rods that formed the first part of the double, climbing with two swift wing beats to take the second with ease. And all the while, as Cara instinctively guided Sky between the rods and poles, another part of her mind was busily analyzing the last obstacle: the triple, the final challenge. *It can't be flown the usual way,* she thought. Breena was right; there's a trick to it. But Breena tried the wrong trick. *What if . . . ?*

And suddenly, Cara knew what she was going to do.

Obstacle followed obstacle in breathtaking succession. Cara was flying in complete harmony with the dragon, as though Sky were an extension of herself. They flew the slalom, missing each pole by a talon's length. For a moment, Cara, grinning madly, was lost in the sensation

of power and rushing speed as
the hazel wands whipped by in a
blur, and sand leapt and twisted into
little dust whorls inches beneath Sky's
flashing wing tips. Then they had
cleared the obstacle, and swung
around the last pylon before the
dreaded triple.

The crowd was utterly silent
now. The spectators held their
breath. The new rider was clear,
so far. Could she . . . ?

Huw reached out involuntarily
and clutched Mistress Hildebrand's arm
with a grip of iron.

Watching from the competitor's
enclosure, Wony bit her clenched fist,
and Drane twisted the hem of his

tunic as if wringing water from it.

Breena, summoned from the paddock by the rumor of unprecedented events in the arena, rushed in to join them, and stared at Skydancer and Cara with tears in her eyes. Hortense gaped, overcome by a rush of incredulity and envy that bid fair to choke her.

Cara guided Skydancer through the last hoop and turned for the triple—but instead of slowing up as Breena and Ernestina had, she sent Sky into a shallow dive, gaining speed.

Breena was appalled. "What's she doing? She's going too fast! She'll never make it. . . ."

Time slowed to a crawl.

Skydancer flew beneath the first rod. The instant he started to climb, he tilted his wings,

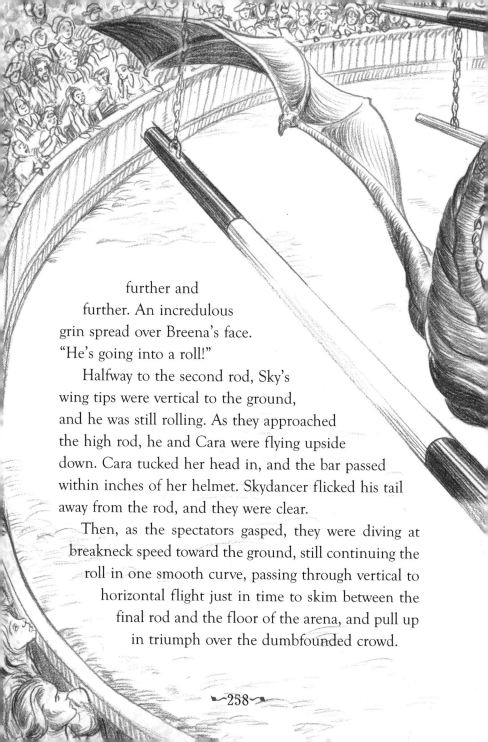

further and
further. An incredulous
grin spread over Breena's face.
"He's going into a roll!"

Halfway to the second rod, Sky's
wing tips were vertical to the ground,
and he was still rolling. As they approached
the high rod, he and Cara were flying upside
down. Cara tucked her head in, and the bar passed
within inches of her helmet. Skydancer flicked his tail
away from the rod, and they were clear.

Then, as the spectators gasped, they were diving at
breakneck speed toward the ground, still continuing the
roll in one smooth curve, passing through vertical to
horizontal flight just in time to skim between the
final rod and the floor of the arena, and pull up
in triumph over the dumbfounded crowd.

"She's clear! She's done
it! She's done it!" Wony, Breena,
and Drane danced around, hugging
and thumping one another on the back,
laughing like maniacs. The stands erupted

with thunderous applause. Huw turned to Mistress Hildebrand and made a gesture of helplessness, which the Chief Riding Instructor failed to notice, being too busy cheering with all the rest.

Hortense stood rooted to the spot for a moment. Then she bowed her head and walked away, quite alone.

And high above the erupting arena, Cara and Skydancer circled—at peace, if only for a moment, with the world and each other.

Cara's appearance put the wyvern among the pigeons in a big way.

The crowd cheered their heads off, demanding that Cara be declared winner of the Intermediate Clear Flight competition. Lord Torin protested vociferously. The judges, after much head-shaking and poring over rule books, decided that Cara could not be awarded the gold rosette on the grounds that she hadn't entered for the event and hadn't paid her entry fee, and that she had completed the course in an improper costume and on a dragon that had already flown it, and that, in any case, belonged to someone else.

All these arguments completely passed Cara by. She stayed in the paddock with Skydancer, hugging and stroking him, talking softly to the dragon while officials tied themselves in knots, and when a deputation of judges came to announce their decision, she simply smiled at them and said, "That's all right. Thank you."

Hortense went around the show ground in a passion, telling anyone who would listen that Skydancer had tried to flame her. But as everyone had seen her inept performance, she had lost all credibility. And when Drane and Wony, the only witnesses to the events that had led to Cara's ride, flatly denied that Skydancer had threatened Hortense in any way, she realized that she was not going to get anywhere and eventually retired to her father's manor in a fine fit of the sulks.

In the interval before the delayed fly-off, Huw came to find Cara. She stood and faced him, perfectly submissive, but determined to apologize for nothing. Perhaps Huw sensed this: At any rate, he delivered no rebuke but merely told his daughter to take the oxcart, which he was ordering back to Dragonsdale immediately.

Cara meekly said good-bye to Skydancer—the parting, though painful, was somehow easier this time—and went.

So it was that at midmorning the following day, Cara was sitting next to the morose driver as the oxcart rumbled through a wide valley when a dragon appeared overhead and swooped in to land. It was Moonflight. Breena alighted and waved. Cara jumped down from the cart and ran to embrace her friend. "What happened in the fly-off?" she cried. "Did you win?"

Breena gave a rueful chuckle. "No. We both faulted at

the last obstacle again, but Ernestina won on time. She pipped me by a few seconds."

Cara groaned with dismay. "Oh, Breena, not again. I'm sorry."

Breena shrugged. "You should have won, anyway, by rights." Cara shook her head. "Oh, well," continued Breena, "you must show me the trick of that roll you did sometime—then we'll see if I can't take Ernestina down a peg."

They both laughed. The cart was some way ahead by now; Breena took Cara's arm and set off to follow it, with Moonflight loping comfortably along behind.

Cara said hesitantly, "So—what about the guard flight?"

Breena shook her head. "If I'd won, Galen would have had no excuse. As it is . . ." She sighed. "He says, maybe next year. . . ." She fell silent as they walked on. After a while, she went on brightly, "We did well in the seniors. A gold, two blues, and a green."

Cara made no reply for a moment. Then she said, "Did you see Sky?"

"Right before I left. I took him a brace of fine fat moorcocks as a treat."

"How was he?"

"All right." Breena gave Cara a sympathetic look. "He wasn't happy, but he seemed—you know—resigned to saying good-bye to you again. Hortense hasn't been anywhere near him, I do know that much. I heard that Torin may be thinking of selling him on."

"Good," said Cara. "He couldn't be any worse off than he was with Hortense."

Hesitantly, Breena asked, "What will you do now?"

Cara sighed. "I don't know. Spend the rest of my life mucking out dragons, I suppose."

"But now your father's seen how well you ride . . ."

"It won't make any difference," said Cara heavily. "He's afraid of me flying, it doesn't matter how well I do it."

"Well, he may change his mind," Breena insisted. "And I know he sold Sky, but you could have another dragon. . . ."

Cara stopped dead, and something in her expression made Breena trail off.

"I don't want another dragon," said Cara. She set off again in the wake of the cart. Breena had to hurry to catch up. "It's over," Cara went on. "I don't suppose I shall ever fly again. It was wonderful while it lasted, but it's over now." Her voice dropped to a whisper. "It's over. . . ."

DRAGONRIDER

On arriving at Dragonsdale House, Cara was surprised to find that her father was still at South Landing. She was not sorry; she had no idea what she and he could have to say to each other on their next meeting, and any delay was welcome.

After greeting Breena, Drane, and Wony, and submitting to a bone-creaking hug from Gerda, Cara slipped away as soon as she could. She lost no time in making her way to her father's study to collect the key to her mother's bedroom. Climbing swiftly up the stairs, she unlocked the door and hurried to the wooden chest containing her mother's possessions.

"Oh, Ma," she whispered, gently running her fingers over the rosettes, sashes, and precious relics of her mother's life.

"You should have seen us. Sky and me . . . You'd have been so proud."

Deep hurt and aching emptiness engulfed Cara as she unfolded the wax cloth to reveal her mother's jacket. She stroked the green material, as if by doing so she could roll back the years and undo the tragedy of the past. Hot tears fell from her eyes onto the jacket, disappearing as the woolen cloth absorbed them, leaving no trace of her sorrow.

She wept for a long time, before an overwhelming sense of injustice took hold of her. Now she had lost the two things she loved most of all. "Sky's gone forever . . ." She buried her face in the soft green cloth and said in muffled tones, "Like you."

A voice behind her said, "I thought I might find you here."

Cara froze. The voice was that of her father. He must have returned soon after her arrival. In her haste, she had failed to lock the door behind her. Her secret had been discovered!

Cara fought to stop her voice from shaking. "I'm sorry, Da. I just wanted to look. It won't happen again."

Her father said, "It's been happening a lot."

Panic rose in Cara's throat. "How . . . ?"

"How do I know? You've been leaving things in the wrong place, or not folded the way you found them."

Guilt and mortification rose through Cara like a flood. She had thought she was being so careful, so secret—but her father had known all the time! She couldn't look at him. She bowed her head.

Then another thought struck, so forcibly she felt her heart skip a beat. How could her father possibly know she'd been careless about putting things back in the box? Unless . . .

She felt the pressure of his hand on her shoulder. In a voice softer than any Cara had ever heard him use, the Dragonmaster said, "Did you think you were the only one who ever opened this box? I come here, too, you know."

Cara looked up in sheer astonishment. Her father came to look in the box, just as Cara did? Huw, the Dragonmaster? The stern, oaken-hearted lord of Dragonsdale, who spoke kindly of no one but dragons and never showed his feelings?

Cara turned to look at her father. He was carrying a rosewood box, which he set down next to the trunk. He produced a key, opened the box, and carefully took out a leather harness with shining silver buckles. Cara stared at them. Silver buckles . . . and two of them were broken. She gasped as a blood-chilling childhood memory came flooding back.

"Mother's . . ."

Her father nodded mournfully and held out the twisted buckles for Cara to see. "Silver . . . beautiful, but not as strong as iron or brass. I should never have let Riona use them. I gave them to her as a present for winning the Bresalian Championship for the third time. It was my fault. . . ."

Cara saw the pain in her father's eyes. Suddenly she understood what had driven him to forbid her to ride Sky or any other dragon. Not just the reason—she had always known that—but the cold, bitter agony of loss and guilt, and the dreadful, numbing fear that one day he could lose his daughter just as he had lost his wife. And, understanding this, Cara could no longer defy him.

In a voice that shook only a little she said, "I'm sorry, Da. I shouldn't have looked in the chest. I shan't do it anymore. And I'll never ride Sky again." A last small spark of longing prompted her to add, "But we flew well together, didn't we?"

Her father remained silent and bowed his head.

Cara turned and walked slowly toward the door. From behind, she heard a soft rustle, and paused just for a moment. Without turning, she knew that her father was holding her mother's flying jacket. Cara didn't look back, unwilling to see the sorrow on his face. She continued toward the door and reached for the latch.

"Cara."

Cara paused dutifully, but she didn't look around.

"You rode well," said Huw, "but you rely too much on your safety belt. It may fail. You must remember to grip harder with your knees next time."

Cara whirled around to face her father, her heart thudding, an expression of wild hope on her face. Next time?

"The new championship season begins in the new year with a showing at Wingover. Can you be ready for it? You and your dragon?"

"My dragon?"

"Well, I couldn't let Lord Torin keep Skydancer after that riding display of yours, could I? And if truth be known, Torin was happy to sell him back to me. I don't think his daughter would want to be near Skydancer ever again."

Cara stood overwhelmed, wide-eyed and speechless.

"Well, don't just stand there. Get down to the stables. Your dragon's waiting for you, no doubt."

With a cry of joy Cara flung her arms around her father. "Thank you, Da, thank you!" Tears once again flooded down her cheeks, but these were tears of joy, not grief. With one final great hug, Cara broke away and headed for the open door, but was pulled up by her father's voice.

"Cara, wait. You're forgetting something."

She turned back quizzically. "What?"

Huw crossed the room and halted in front of Cara. He held out her mother's green show jacket. "You'll be needing this—dragonrider."

The next few minutes passed in a blur. Putting on the precious jacket and once again hugging her father, Cara galloped downstairs and rushed out of the house. She ran across the cobbles of the stable yard. Before her, clustered together and grinning for all they were worth, stood Mistress Hildebrand, Breena, Wony, and Drane, and, wings held aloft, rearing up proudly in their midst, Skydancer.

"Sky!" shouted Cara in utter joy.

The dragon was tacked up and ready to fly. Cara's friends stood aside to let her past, and she threw herself at her beloved Skydancer, hugging him and stroking his muzzle for all she was worth. Sky gave a joyful chirrup and crooned.

With a multitude of thank-yous, Cara bounded up into the saddle, helped by a smiling Breena and Drane. Huw appeared in the doorway to the kitchen, accompanied by Gerda. Mistress Hildebrand handed Cara the reins with the exhortation, "Fly well!"

Cara pulled back on the reins, urging Sky upward. Gerda put a reassuring arm around Huw's shoulders, and Breena, Drane, Wony, and Mistress Hildebrand waved as the dragon gave a triumphant cry and a beat of his wings, which lifted him and Cara effortlessly into the air.

If this was a story, thought Cara, *the sun would be setting, and we'd be flying off into it.*

But it wasn't. The sun was high in the sky, blazing out over the Isles of Bresal, and together, Cara and Skydancer rose to meet it.

DRAGON LOG

DOCUMENT OF DESCRIPTION FOR THE
IDENTIFICATION OF GOLDENBROW DRAGONS.
ISSUED ON BEHALF OF THE BRESALIAN DRAGON
BREEDING AUTHORITY, DRAGON HOUSE,
SOUTH LANDING, BRESAL

NAME OF DRAGON:

Skydancer

BREED:

Goldenbrow

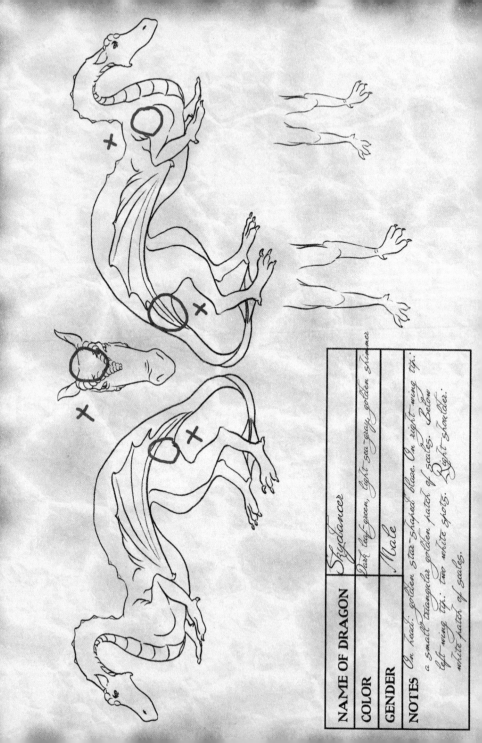

NAME OF DRAGON	Skydancer
COLOR	Dark leaf-green, light sea-gray, golden shimmer
GENDER	Male
NOTES	On head: golden star-shaped blaze. On right wing tip: a small triangular golden patch of scales. Below left wing tip: two white spots. Right shoulder: white patch of scales.

GOLDENBROW DRAGON

The Goldenbrow is the rarest of all dragon types. It is closest genetically to its wild ancestors; thus, while strong, durable, and resistant to many common diseases, it is the hardest type with which to establish a human Trustbond.

Training a Goldenbrow tends to be a long and difficult process, as they are typically obstinate and self-willed. However, a Goldenbrow that accepts a rider will prove a loyal and brave companion.

The Goldenbrow combines many of the best features of other breeds. They are excellent fliers, fast yet maneuverable. They are also hardy, adaptable, and highly intelligent.

NAME OF DRAGON	Skydancer
OWNER	Huw of Dragonsdale
DATE OF HATCHING	Midwinter of the year 955 of the Trustbond
ISLAND OF HATCHING	Seahaven
STABLE	Dragonsdale
GENDER	Male
SIRE	Unknown
DAME	Unknown wild dragon
GRAND SIRE	Unknown
GRAND DAME	Unknown
ADDITIONAL NOTES	Found as a hatchling.
	Mother found dead. Father unknown.

DATE OF EXAMINATION *19th day of Midwinter of the year 955*

SIGNATURE OF EXAMINING DRAGONLEECH

Bresalian Dragon Breeding Authority

TRAINING LOG: *Skydancer*

SKILL:	DATE EXAMINED:
Flying with reins	4th Frostide, 957

REMARKS:

A waste of time! The dragon refused a head harness and ate the reins!

Signature of instructor:	*Hildebrand*

SKILL: Flying to a lure	DATE EXAMINED: 27th Harvestide, 957

REMARKS:

Fat chance! Ignored the lure and chased his handler into the Dragonsmere. A complete fiasco.

Signature of instructor:	*Hildebrand*

SKILL: Being saddled	DATE EXAMINED: 4th Lambingtide 958

REMARKS:

Set fire to saddle and went and perched on roof of house until Cara was able to persuade the dragon down. This is beyond a joke!

Signature of instructor:	*Hildebrand*

SKILL:	DATE EXAMINED:
Being saddled (again!)	16th Midsummer, 958

REMARKS:

Took to the air while stable hand was trying to fasten saddle belt! Dragon extremely agitated (though not as agitated as stable hand). Dragon later taken to Alberich with set fast. It is my belief he is shamming.

Signature of instructor:	*Hildebrand*

SKILL:	DATE EXAMINED:
Flying a small show course	No Point

REMARKS:

If this dragon ever succeeds in flying any show course, I'll eat my riding boots! I wash my hands of this beast!

Signature of instructor:	*Hildebrand*

SKILL:	DATE EXAMINED:
Clear round in the Island Championships!	Now!

REMARKS:

Extraordinary transformation. Cara has her mother's gift. A true Trustbond! Where will they go next?

Signature of instructor:	*Hildebrand*